Storm Over Sydney

Jeanell Buckley

Storm Over Sydney

Ginninderra Press published Jeanell Buckley's novella *Stretcher Bearer* in 2018, and her poem 'At the Lookout' in the collection *Mountain Secrets* in 2019. Jeanell completed this short story collection *Storm Over Sydney*, but died in 2021.

Contents

1

Bondi

Rolf had spilt orange juice on the front of his shorts. Bastard stuff. He hated health drinks, and this one was a health drink in his book. Blast the lot of them – the doctors, Hilda and those kids who seemed to know it all.

The road had cooled down and the wind was high. Tanny tugged at her lead and dragged him left then right, hearing the drain under the road, smelling the cats, the rising sweetness of the sandy earth with its ants and rotting leaves. He wouldn't go far. The beach was only a half a mile away but he'd do as he was told. So it would be the back and forth under the trees, turning back at the curve near the Baths. They were digging it all up for some works, always some new thing down there. If he'd gone into cement, he'd be a billionaire by now.

They'd made a mess of the old house at the end of the road. The rose bush was gone, the low veranda with the old couch was naked with its weathered timbers exposed. It used to have a cat on it, a scraggy ginger fellow that Tanny liked the look of. The guy he'd seen there was not a bad type, an old wog like him. He'd sometimes tried a word of Croatian on him and got silence, the long glance as he walked away. Stupid old man, he'd muttered to himself, what did you think you were doing trying to make friends at your age? Still, they kept up the nods, the pale smiles, the odd word about Tanny. Another dog man, under the thumb of his cat lover wife.

So in a week, a glass and steel double storey would be there. The old man wasn't there any more. Now it was the young couple he'd seen popping in and out, quick with glinting sunglasses as they rushed from their big car. He wondered about the old man, supposed the kids had put him in some home. Or he was dead, lucky bastard.

He was finding the descent the hardest, downward curving footpath, the fear of falling creeping up on him over the last weeks. The sun close to the horizon, blinding off the footpath, specks of sand, pools eddying down to the eroded cliff, a run-off from a broken gutter. Bikes didn't help. Kids zoomed onto the road, risking their lives dodging bodies and big dogs on leads as they headed down to the coast walk. Somewhere down a drive, he heard a skateboard rattle, a woman calling from a back balcony. Let them be, he thought. Not your problem now.

The wind was warming him already. Turning into Bondi Road, he felt the reflection, the sun soaking in, hitting him from the top of the cars and the sheen of the thinning clouds. A pair of lovers separated to make room for him at the fruit shop. The boy smiled down at the roadway as if he had something to hide. They are too polite, these Aussies. One day, their country will be taken from them and they won't know what hit them.

'Ah, Rolf. A coffee, mate?' The fat Italian who ran the deli had seen him.

He smiled back, reluctant to linger because he couldn't stay out too long because of Hilda. She worried. Her grizzled mouth was the burden he carried along the path of his life.

'Hello, there.' He raised his hand in reply.

Tanny let out a short bark of recognition and headed to the deli. A girl on a mobile phone stood up to give him her chair. Did he look that old? Yes, he must, the drool of juice on his shorts a confirmation of it.

'A few clouds around,' the man said.

'Summer,' he answered.

He knew he should sit but continued to stand, bow-legged, a pest in the path of women shuffling past with their kid's lunch supplies. Bulging bags with the shop's name on the side.

Someone in a German car idled in the near lane, deaf to the angry horns behind him, his eyes fixed on the road ahead as if his next ten minutes were all that mattered in the world.

He remembered a tank driver, a tough sod everyone hated, impassive behind goggles while his buddies fried next to him. Still the Tommies got him in the end. He could scream with the best of them with the skin sizzling off his face.

'How's the wife, mate?'

'Not bad, mate.' A word he hated using. It was too familiar. He was always an imposter using it, hiding within his Australian shell.

He remembered everything, this Italian. Rolf wasn't sure about him. Why didn't he just get back to work?

Back in the shop, those kids behind the counter were scowling. They wanted to be at some bar or at the beach. If he owned this shop, he'd get rid of any kid who didn't greet every customer. The Italian was too kind to them, or maybe he was worried they'd make a fuss, get some lawyer friend to write some threatening letter.

'You going home this year?' the Italian asked.

'Maybe. Not sure. Depends…' he pointed to his leg.

'Knee?'

Of course the bloody knee, but what word was it? It might come to him later, but maybe not. Every week he lost another one, words which he'd never fully grafted onto his brain strongly enough in the first place.

'Operation went well,' he said instead. 'Now, time to wait. See if it takes.'

The Italian nodded, brought him a coffee whether he wanted it or not.

Tanny's lead was caught in the aluminium leg of a chair. Some confusion as the Italian scraped the leg free. A German tourist paused at the door to the café and yelled at her old man, who was lagging behind. Rolf tried not to look too hard at them. He'd kept his distance from other Germans. They scratched at the sore inside him. He tugged Tanny close to his side. When the Italian smiled at them, he made a gruff farewell and walked on.

Not getting enough sun this summer had left him grumpy. Hilda would say it was the leg, giving him trouble all night, the grinding as he rose from bed each morning like the cogs of the cuckoo clock his parents had owned. The mood would settle on him if he didn't punch through it. Defiant, he walked on and further than he should. Past the bottle shop and some new club. Inside, the lights were murky like a wet night, bottles lining the walls high just for show. Nightclubs used to gleam like the stars. Now it was all about blurring things.

He hadn't drunk wine since Natalie's wedding. A longing grew between his shoulder blades at the thought of her, an angel in that wedding dress of shimmering silk. It'd been months since he'd held his little girl. Still overseas, taking that boy of hers on some mercy mission to dig holes in Africa. He hadn't rested since she'd left. At the thought of Africa, flies swarmed in his mind and ate at his dreams, a mine buried in his mind sprang to life again, and there was Natalie wandering through the treacherous sands.

A van roared past, then slammed on brakes as it met traffic. A surfboard protruded from the back. The sea brooded ahead, its surface faintly rippled by the late wind, a twisting current running across it. He thought of the sand and felt cold.

Tanny sped ahead, the tug of her lead making him shuffle faster than he liked. She was still young. In days past, he'd let her off to run down, the wind skimming along her little sides. No more. The government had nothing better to do than pick on dogs and litterers. Meanwhile, the drunks came and went from the big hotel down at the beach. He could hear them from where he was, the other end of the bay, the disco throb reminding him of mortar fire.

He thought of Natalie again but pushed her away. She was an adult, she must make her way with the boy now. Hilda prayed for the baby to come, but Rolf didn't believe the two of them, nodding, saying they'd try straight away. And maybe they were right. What was the point of more kids to make a path to their own death?

He'd gone too far, and was down near the Icebergs. A little girl with a bike and helmet wanted to pat Tanny, but he hurried forward to get away. Tanny could snap. The father was close behind the little girl, an adult echo of the child with his own plastic helmet and the bike. These men never grew up.

'Dad, look, she likes me!'

Tanny sniffed.

'What's her name?

He told her, holding the lead tight.

The dog dribbled onto the footpath. The girl's shoes were the pink of musk sticks he used to buy for Natalie at the corner shop after school. The shop was gone now, had become a dry cleaners, plastic bags holding coats, men's laundered shirts swooped in circles where the glass counter used to be. The Saturday afternoons, taking Natalie and the neighbour's boy to the park with a cricket bat. He did his best to run their little bodies to exhaustion.

This little girl in the pink stayed close to Tanny. He thought she'd speak to him again, waited, recognised the neediness within himself and felt the shame of it.

'She's a good little girl,' he said at last, thinking of them both, two girls looking at the world with nothing but joy in their eyes.

'I want a dog,' the child said, looking at him.

'Come on, Sal, better get a move on. You're blocking the road.' The father half laughed. Thought himself considerate, no doubt. They killed joy with their deference.

Tanny didn't care. She'd wandered as far as she could across in front of other kids, power walkers with plugs in their ears and those devices in their hands.

Wind from the beach was sticky, a sultry whoosh of waves washed the ocean pool. Traffic was building and soon people were stepping into traffic, the slow crawl of weekenders going home.

The little girl kept chasing Tanny and her father started raising his voice.

'Sally!'

It worked. The little girl obeyed. A parent's command counted. Together, they were off then, Tanny left behind.

Tanny saw the beach and strained towards the sand. A year earlier,
a sleepy winter morning with mist on the grass, he'd let her off the lead
and she'd caught a rat and proudly dropped it at his feet. Sand, blood,
animal shit – his shoes collected it, but he didn't care. Hilda would have
scolded if he'd brought it in. She scrubbed her tiled kitchen every day.
They'd told him he'd regret marrying a woman so many years younger
than him, but he had no complaints – she was a good wife. There was
no running in the sands today. Anyway, the crowds were too big. Everyone wanted something of the summer before it was too late. Warm
air came and went as the sun peeked from churning clouds. He knew
he should turn back, but Tanny kept looking up at him. She was thirsty
and so was he.

In no time at all, they were on the parade, the cracking cement
under him, the graffiti a jagged growth in his peripheral vision. Tanny
wanted to run, she tugged, he felt his knees start to tremble. She was
like Natalie, impatient to be free of the old man. The thought was
enough to make him hurry. He felt his stupidity spreading up his stiff
limbs but couldn't stop himself. Crowds of kids, skateboarders above
hitting the low walls of the parade with the wheels, strollers with plastic
bags looped over the handles, flapping, crackling in the wind. A skinny
boy held a little surfboard and flew around him spraying sand and sea
water.

'Bloody kids,' he cursed under his breath.

A tap dribbled ahead and, with a single determined lunge, Tanny
was away, her lead dragging along the parade.

'Tanny! Tanny!'

People were looking. An old fool pleading with his dog. He wanted
Hilda beside him. But Hilda was at home, sprawled out in the chair on
the back porch sucking on peppermints and reading the paper. Maybe
Ricka from down the road had come up and together they'd be talking
in German, letting their vocal cords relax back into the old tongue.

A boy had grabbed Tanny's lead and was reining her in, patting her little head as she slurped at the tap mouth. She drank as they used to during the war, like starving mules, plunging their snouts into the puddles made by the tanks.

The boy smiled up at him, his eyes hidden behind sunglasses, a swath of black hair flopping across his forehead and down to the rim of his T-shirt. Metal in his nose, some scrawl across the T-shirt which might have been English or might not.

'She's a sweetie,' the boy said. His slender fingers scratched at the top of her head.

Rolf nodded, suppressed his relief that Tanny was safe. He told himself not to think of Natalie wandering in the sand, her little legs bare and forever young to him. Jealousy of the boy, that was it. No, anger. That this son-in-law of his could be so reckless with his daughter. He must let it go. It must be that man's duty now to protect her whether he liked it or not.

Sweat ran on the back of his neck. He'd never make it back now. His legs were trembling. Hilda would come and look for him in the car, would get a traffic ticket for parking in a no standing zone. His fault, so often his fault. This old age had castrated his place in that household. Leaning with his palm against the wall, he watched the dog drink, with the boy crouched beside her. A grey line on the horizon had thickened to the colour of fresh steel. He smelt salt, Tanny's rising heat, some steak on the barbecue at the back of the pub. Suddenly he felt sick.

'Is he all right?' a female voice said.

The boy had a girl with him, wearing a mere nightie of a dress, red dyed hair, boots polished like stormtroopers. She was pretty – why wear such things? They didn't know their luck, their fresh clean faces unlined.

'You all right, mate?' The boy held Tanny in his arms now. The dog licked the pale hairs on his hands.

'Put her down!' the girl whispered, the child wanting out of trouble. 'He doesn't like it.'

'It's OK,' Rolf said at last. 'Come, Tanny.' He started to move off back the other way along the parade.

A throbbing sound system coming from one of the cafés assaulted his ears. Their eyes were burrowing through his back as he tried to distance himself from them. Their watching left a gulf of silence which followed him along the parade. Then the nausea, his collapsing legs, his aching knee. Unable to stop it, he leant into the wall again. The ground was wet, Tanny sniffed around water running to a drain.

'Want some help, mister?'

The kids were at his side again, their sweet young faces pale as lambs. They brought tears to him which he rubbed away. He could draw them both into his chest and hold them, pour the warmth of his strength into them as he used to after the park games years ago, the cricket sweat a mingling of healthy humanity, Natalie's little hand touching his waist, her tickling spidering grasp.

He let them walk beside him. The boy made babble about the day, some storm coming, the girl kissed Tanny, letting the dog drool onto her dress.

And then he was in the boy's car, the front seat, the girl and Tanny smiling forward in the side mirror. Sunlight sliced between buildings, flickering into his eyes, off the cliffs at the southern end of the beach, the yellow walls of the big houses. A gush of cold wind hit him as they rumbled up the hill.

'I'm Ashe,' the boy said. 'This is Jo.'

He gave them his name. The car was an old one. It gurgled in the choked traffic. The deep seat reminded him of his first Australian car, a long Ford that he and Hilda would take lazy rides down to Wollongong in, picnicking at the side of the dirt roads. The blessed days and simple freedoms of Australia.

'I could walk. It is not far.'

'It's fine, you were…' old, the boy wanted to say. He hunched over the wheel, which was designed for a larger man than him. 'You were off colour. Can't walk home like that.'

'And Ashe should know, he's a nurse, and…'

'Well, nearly.' He chuckled. 'A year yet.'

'Yeah, but you know, like, you can see when someone's not all right.' She was alarmed she might have caused offence. 'Like sick, that's all. He's a natural, all the other staff at the hospital say so.'

'Oh yeah, right.'

They babbled on. Boys as nurses made no sense to him, this boy with a nonsense name, but he said nothing. The girl put her painted toes against the back of his seat, the boy Ashe chewed gum, Yank style, with his mouth open. They giggled as Tanny peered through the back window. The boy pumped the brake too hard, hesitating at traffic lights before forging loudly through. Reckless, strangers to fear. At least Natalie was sensible. She'd always had a head on her shoulders, two university degrees and a husband by thirty not a bad score.

He pointed to his street and the boy turned down the narrow roadway, the huge car growing more audible under the trees. The asphalt was drying from the earlier rain, but thick drops were thudding onto the windscreen. The remains of tree fruit, blackening to syrup, squelched under the tyres. The girl got out an umbrella, seemed to think he'd need one to walk the twenty yards to his door. Thunder was rolling from the sea, and the wind had dropped. He was an hour late, Hilda would be peering from behind the curtains. There'd be questions, introductions, more talk from the kids, while the huge car parked crooked across a driveway of the apartment block next door with everyone watching.

He thanked them hurriedly. Tanny was circling at the girl's feet wanting to be picked up again. He felt a sudden guilt for not holding her more, she loved it so.

'You right from here on?' the boy asked. Sunglasses raised onto his forehead, that soft smile at odds with the hardness of his hair, the nose ring, the angry smear across the T-shirt.

'Oh, Ashe, what the…' The girl was looking at her phone, her mouth open with panic. 'The time, man! It's 3.48!'

'Oops!' The boy winked at him, scooped back into the cabin of the car. 'Gotta go. Bye.'

'His twenty-first. Only a month late.'

'I only got back last night,' he continued to Rolf, leaning from the window. 'Been in Cambodia a year.'

He made a smile for them, a churning in his weak stomach. Hunger? No, he was too old for that. A flutter, as he felt in Italy that day fifty-five years ago when his unit had surrendered. A gratefulness at the comfort of sun on his face and air in his lungs.

'But we're glad to be back!' The girl had moved to the front seat and had her feet on the dashboard.

The car reversed.

Leaning over suddenly, Rolf grabbed the open window frame. He felt its heat slice through to his bones. 'I am Rolf,' he said. 'Come some-time for a coffee.'

The girl Jo nodded, they waved.

'Bye!' she yelled.

Then they were gone.

The roar of the car was replaced by the drip drip of raindrops on the fig leaves and the small roof of the mailbox. The little panting from Tanny's mouth was sweet in his ears as he leant to lift her. He knew he shouldn't, he wasn't allowed to bend, but he didn't care. But squirming from his arms, she was soon off the leash and dashing up to the porch. Hilda's moon face was peering into the gloom of the dusk from the front window. He smiled to himself and wondered why. Natalie would be in Athens by now, no doubt some fancy hotel the boy had booked with a pool on the roof.

He thought of the boy in the car with the strange name. By the boy's age, he had gone to war, had killed men. The boy with his pale pure flesh, the girl's little feet on the dash, he should have kissed them both, should have held them like the babies they were.

He put the light on and Hilda shoved a towel at his feet to stop the water. She watched him stow away the lead, hobble to the couch, then called the police and cancelled the alarm. The smell of cabbage and roast meat filled the flat. Lorikeets started to carry on out on the balcony where the rain was heavy. Water bounced off the rail, clouds had made it like night out there. Such colour, the eerie deep green of the birds and the fig tree, the rumble of thunder rolling in again. Such light, he thought he'd entered a dream. Maybe the drugs and the heat, something inside him had been turned up. He knew the beach would be awash now, slippery, stinging sand in his face. He had made it home safely. A sigh escaped him and when the thought of Natalie came to him he pushed it away. It did her no good, and she wouldn't be thinking of him, lounging in that pool on the other side of the world.

He thought instead of toes and of the first time he'd tasted chewing gum – he'd been seventeen and just joined the army. It was the sweetest thing he'd ever known. A roast was splattering against the walls of the oven. It would be as tough as horse, but he was used to it. When Hilda spoke, he let her go on. She did no harm. He was surprised to realise he wanted to be nowhere else on earth.

2

Dee Why

Hot days have never been Valerie's thing. She has flaky skin, thin lips, hair the colour of dusty straw. She's seen girls of her complexion with blisters on their eyelids, but she's never been that stupid. Back then, Mattie liked a tan. Well, everyone did. A good skin-shedding was a sign of duty done under the sun. If you did it right, you got tanned. If you didn't, or chickened out after two scorchers, you stayed red and flaky.

She sees Mattie. At first, she isn't sure if it's him. This guy has a wide hefty middle, a sloped back. He hunches at the edge of the car park on the kerb. There's a Coke can at his side, scuffed work shoes on his toes.

'Mattie!' She half yells it across the car park.

There are only two cars there. A ute (must be Mattie's), and a four-wheel drive with a wardrobe of clothes thrown in the back.

'It's me!'

He hasn't recognised her. He's searching her face, shading his eyes from the sun. Then a smile. 'Oh, hi.' As if it's only been a couple of hours. 'Great day, huh.'

'What are you doing here?'

He shrugs.

'Just hanging out?' she asks. What a let-off. She should make him speak first. Make him admit to her that the boat business he'd dreamed of had never come off and that, instead, he spends his weekdays mowing lawns at the surf club with a stained T-shirt and boobs larger than hers. He'd never been good with words, so some things never changed. She supposes she should feel sorry for him. 'Yeah, me too. Been up on the headland. Gorgeous views. I'd forgotten.'

'Walking?'

'Kind of. Didn't bring the right shoes, you see.' Giggling, she indicates her expensive pumps. Christ, how easy it is to fake inanity. 'In fact, I wasn't expecting to get here at all. But I finished up earlier than I expected in Acacia Drive. I was in the area on business. Up there – you know the street?' She flicks her head up towards the houses, indicating the street on the escarpment where every house has floor to ceiling glass and security gates.

He wipes his Coke-stained hand against his shorts. 'Right. Well, whatever, you look great.'

'You reckon?'

'Oh, yeah!'

She suppresses a snort of derision. She knows she does. Appearance matters in her business. Well, when doesn't it matter?

Cicadas are pulsing down in the dunes. If she hadn't had business close by, she'd never have come within a mile of this surf club. If she hadn't finished the job early, she'd never have walked this way. If she hadn't spotted him… She should just walk away. But what the hell?

The elastic's gone from Mattie's shorts and he looks like he's forgotten how to tie his shoe laces. Brain damage from the grog? No, he'd always been a bit slobby, but back then it'd been endearing in an uncouth way.

'Mattie, this is too much,' she exclaims a bit too cheerfully. 'Too many years!'

'Tell me about it!'

'You still live around here?'

'Hmm, no… I can't afford…' His words trail off.

'But your parents?'

'They're around, I dunno where… What about you?'

'Not here.' She lets her smile drop but he doesn't pick up on it.

That sun's getting hot. She wouldn't be surprised to see rain later. It's the time of day she hates most. Her skin itches. She'd let this guy rub suntan oil on her more times than she cares to remember. Basting her for the bloody barbecue as if she were a cut of steak.

'Nice here at the beach,' he says.

'Always your place, Mattie – I can't picture you anywhere else.',

'Oh yeah. Always on my best at the beach.' He trundles to the garbage bin in his loose shoes. 'You can't help it. It makes you…fresh, cleared out somehow. When I'm away, I miss it.'

'Really. What parts do you miss?' She feels her voice turn to steel.

'Oh, I dunno. I feel kinda young here. It makes me feel young again.'

'I was young here too.'

'Yeah.' He nods like it's only just dawned on him. 'Yeah, and it was great – wasn't it?'

She wonders if she's misheard him. Did he really say that? 'You finished here?' she asks. 'Work, I mean?'

'Shit, yeah.' He scoffs at the abandoned lawnmower. Maybe if she's lucky, he'll get sacked.

'Let's look at the beach. It's over there, isn't it?' She makes a show of remembering, but only a moron would miss it.

They walk side by side along the sand trail. It's been widened, and there are only a couple of spots where they have to cuddle up close.

'I was never one for swimming. Remember? Couldn't stand the sand in my hair. Besides, all those nits used to set off my allergies.'

'Oh, yeah. The insects.'

'That's the beach for you,' she says, finding it easy to blame nature. 'Full of bloody pests.'

When they reach it, the sun has started to go down, so at least she's spared the heat. There were five of them on the beach that last time, she and another girl called Mandy, and the boys. She can't remember the names of the boys. It seems odd but maybe it isn't really. If she saw them far off, coming towards her in the street, passing her in the aisles of the supermarket…

'I can't surf now.' He's confiding to her in a wistful murmur. 'Shoulder. Did it in football and never got fixed. Not right somehow.'

'And you let that stop you surfing? Sounds a bit lame.'

He starts, blinks at her, as if she's flickering a torch into his eyes. 'The pain – it catches you. When you least expect it.'

Didn't she know it. 'Well, still. Bet the others are still going out. A bit of footy wouldn't stop them.'

This makes him squirm and there it is unchanged, that sullen hunch of his again. For a second, she sees the old Mattie, sulking, ready to throw a punch at his best friend. He was never tall, but his stomach used to be as hard as corrugated iron, the whole shape of him thick with muscle, his very toes squeezing the juice from the grass under him.

'Yeah, well,' he says, 'like I said, it catches you. I know a guy who drowned out there. Shit, what a mess.' Leaning against the thick post of the dunes, his shirt comes loose and she sees his flabby waist. Coke is drying brown on his shirt. Then he looks at her, almost pleading. 'He had a pain – in his gut. Ignored it, like.' He waits for her to nod and she obliges. This is encouragement enough to go on. 'You gotta be careful. I mean it, the surf can be mean. Real mean. There was another guy too – older one. His board ripped his shoulder right through – had to be pulled back like a…like a rag in the washing. He told me. At least that wasn't me. At least…'

'So you've been careful. You've kept yourself out of trouble all these years.'

'What?' As if he's forgotten she's there. 'Have I?'

'You tell me. Any problem with the cops?'

'Why? What sort of problem?' His mouth hangs open, flesh pooling in loops under his chin.

She remembers that mouth, it used to have muscles too. 'You'd know.'

'You said something, the cops.'

'Just wondering. You were a wild lot. All of you.'

'Oh yeah, sure.' This reminder comforts him, but only for so long. 'But the cops. What about them?'

'How would I know?' She wishes she still smoked. It's awkward feeling the air cool around them and nothing to do with her hands. She's left her bag back in the car. When night fell, that car park used to be break-in paradise. If she had her bag, she'd hold its warm leather against her heart. 'You wouldn't be the first guy to have cop trouble. Agreed?'

'Hmm, suppose. I see 'em round. You know.'

'What. Watching you?'

'Dunno.'

'Who then? If not you?'

'Why me? What have I done? They come to the club sometimes. They want free drinks, I guess. But me, why would I be…?'

'Only you'd know, Mattie.'

Fuck, she feels like the cops. She's towering over him. How has she grown taller over thirteen years and he's shrunk? That doesn't happen. Maybe the sand dune, maybe the way it slopes away, into the tide, not even the same sand they sunk into thirteen years ago. She finds herself looking, looking out over it. Where did it happen?

'Look, Mattie, you can ask yourself lots of questions. Maybe you haven't. I have. Lots of them. Even… If maybe I… Oh, what the fuck, Mattie!'

It comes out in a kind of scream. It makes him back away, he's slipping into sand, losing his balance, fumbling with an outstretched hand for the rail. She hopes that as his palm slips over it he catches a splinter. Finally he does fall, and his splayed legs reveal the full expanse of his loose thighs.

'I…I don't get it,' he mumbles. 'You…are you… Look, if you've got a problem… Like I'll help you. I really will.'

'A problem after thirteen years?' He was right in a way, she did have a problem. 'And if I did, whose fault would that be? Well?'

'Urrh, sand.' He slips as he tries to rise.

Sand clings at him. He reaches out as if she's going to help him up. Like a toddler with his mum in the sandpit. The air is turning cold and rain spits at her face, but she feels heat pulsing out of her. Spray is settling into a haze along the beach. She doesn't want to look for the spot now.

'Yeah, the sand, Mattie. You liked it back then. Couldn't get enough of it. It was your natural environment, like a lizard or something.'

'Yeah, maybe. Look…I gotta go.'

He's hurrying back now along the track and she pursues him, grasping, tugging at any of him she can. Rain runs down his head and splits his hair into tubes the size of leeches. He's not leaving before he acknowledges what he did. She's reminded of an Italian film where a nagging wife chases her husband down an alley. The husband's the hero, the wife the shrew. At the end, she's been dropped from the story. There's only so long a man can bear a screaming woman.

'Stop now, Mattie. Right now! Don't you dare run from me!'

'No!' He's keeping up a laboured jog, wailing as he goes. 'I'm not listening to you! I'm not!'

The stupid dick's afraid of her. She takes that realisation and tucks it away to savour later, but for now she's angry.

'You prick, you treated me like rubbish back there, remember? Yes, you forced me to…'. She knew the word for it, but it had been buried too long within her to be unearthed again.

'No…' he's saying, his voice high and whiny. 'No.'

'You did – whether you think you did or not. Forced me to do it to you, then you passed me to the others. I was a fucking piece of meat to you.'

The rain obliterates his voice. It is melting her inside.

'Mattie – don't you dare run away from me!'

The trail is too long. Her pumps are the problem. She drags them off and throws them in among the bushes. She did something like that before with her clothes thirteen years ago, then shuffled half nude along the road under the moon's perfect circle. High tide then, and the surf roaring from every cliff edge. They'd had a fire going down there with fish and pineapple and grog, all of them calling out for her to come back and have some, laughing, Mattie the loudest. The smell of barbecued pineapple could still turn her stomach.

Back at the surf club there's only one car in the forlorn car park – the four-wheel drive. Lights appear in the bleak headland behind. He's dragging the mower across the cement because it's quicker that way to the open roller door of the shed, the metal scrapes along the ground in a blunt scream. He's breathing hard.

'Feeling picked on are you, Mattie? Poor Mattie.'

'Shut up, you.'

'Worried about your job, are you? Or rust or something on your little toy?'

Her breath is heaving within her. He keeps working. She should leave now, but can't. It feels too good to pour bile over him. She wants to bury him in it, even if it'll never be enough.

'It's not too late to call the cops, you know. Maybe I will, who knows? You'll find out, I guess.'

'Cops? Who?'

She laughs, smooth as she can make it. He really has a problem with that word. It's a storm now, lightning flashes over the sea. He blinks, shrinks from it. Christ, she used to love him once.

'You're pathetic,' she says.

'Yeah, well better than mad. Like you, lady, off the planet.'

'If I am, well – I'll blame you again. It's not your day, is it?'

'I'll make you shut up now.' He's finished with the shed. He's marching off to the office.

There's a moment when all she can hear is the thunder and the water on her head and she's frightened. Maybe he's getting a knife or a cricket bat to hit her with. He was always one for a solid blunt instrument in his hand. She'd seen him use one on his best friend. It seemed to be always on his best friends. She thought they'd been friends of a kind once.

When he comes out, he has someone with him. One of the club oldies.

'Can I help you?' he asks.

Mattie is hiding behind him, literally cowering behind the guy's back. There's a smell of fresh urine.

'This is private,' she says as calmly as she can. 'I need to talk to him.'

'Mattie can't talk any more. He's going home now.'

'What do you mean he can't talk? Look, will you just leave, please?' Her knees are trembling. She needs a whisky and a bath. Her top is sodden and dragging at her. 'He's big enough to face me alone.'

'Mattie doesn't know you, young lady.'

'Like hell! And don't call me young lady.' She's taking it out on him, letting it spill into men generally, like she used to before she got sorted out. If only she'd called the cops thirteen years ago.

'I'm going now and Mattie's going with me.' He starts to walk away. 'I'm sorry, the club is closed. Goodnight.'

'You're giving him a ride away, are you?'

'I give him a lift every day. He can't drive on his own.'

'What, always plastered by the end of the day, is he?' She scoffs, feels the sound rebound off the darkening trees. She hates those mean shrubs.

'No, he can't drive… But it's not that.' Reaching behind him, he takes Mattie by the hand, by his sticky Coke-smeared hand, and leads him to the car.

The smell of urine comes to her on the wind. What the…?

With his car open, the old guy gets a towel and wraps it round Mattie's middle. Her skin shivers at the sight of the two of them illuminated in the internal light of the car.

'You'd better leave…miss…' He looks up at the bastard. 'I don't have her name, Mattie. She hasn't said it, has she?'

Mattie shakes his head. He is shuddering, his jaw wobbling with cold.

'I don't know it either.' He's peering at her through the deluge.

'But this is crap. He knows me. He can't pretend. We've been talking. He knew me years ago.'

'No, he doesn't know you.'

'But we've just walked to the beach. I mentioned the police – he knows them well enough.'

'Oh yes, I'm sure he agreed with you. He would. It's how he gets by.' He looks up at her, his mouth a wry smile. 'He forgets, you see… So pretending helps.'

He has spare socks for Mattie. He seems to have spare of everything for Mattie.

'So you're his best mate then.'

'The best he'll ever have – his father.'

And there was that same lazy eye in the man's head as he blinked water away, the same stub-shaped ear which she used to pull at and call cute. What a little girl she'd been.

'But he said…' She is yelling into the car window, her wet hands clutching the edge of the door. 'So…he lives with you then. Since the footy accident.'

'Since the car crash. The footy accident was mine, I'm afraid. Twisted shoulder. I don't surf any more. Pity. I had life membership at the club.' He starts up the car, and checks Mattie's seatbelt. 'Goodnight, young lady.' He starts to raise the window to keep the rain and her out. 'I have to close this now.' He swallows and wipes at his wet forehead.

Her instinct is to ram her closed fist into his smug face as the glass rises. As they turn into the road, she catches Mattie's eye. In his face is a fleeting terror. As the car accelerates, she grabs at the handle, feels her hands slip in the rain, and she's on the ground. It is hitting her now, the rain from above her and the car park beneath her. Her head side on, she sees the pools gather, the running away of sand and, at the horizon, the blackness of the storm rolling inland.

There is a roar somewhere – it is a wave crashing down at the beach. Then a bruised rumble of churning sand and tide ripping the shore apart. That beach is gone, that sand from years ago washed away long ago back out to sea and forgotten. For a second, she forgets who she is, what year it is, how she got there. There is no sun, there is no moon. There is nothing above her but a maelstrom at the edge of the world which is blind to her.

She crawls to her knees and then to her feet, then stumbles towards the path through the sands. The roar grows. She stumbles down the dunes and onto the beach. The wind tugs at her and she sinks into a flooded channel. It is over there somewhere. She crawls and lets the rain batter her until her mind has been scrubbed raw with its fury. Then she knows she has reached the place.

3

Chinatown

I'd been planning to get the train out to Ashfield with the Christmas sales crowd. The air conditioning had been up so high that when I hit the platform at Central I thought I'd stepped off a plane in Jakarta. The smell of oily bread and fried chicken hung in the railway concourse. I'd put on a linen shirt I knew the old man would like. My hair was combed and I'd run a damp towel over the tips of my brown shoes and left them with a gleam good enough for the school photo. I'd been running my own show for five years after leaving the police and this was my first job with a Chinese family. Waiting for the tram, I pushed my nervous energy down through my middle toes and out to the pavement. My mum's t'ai chi lessons come in handy sometimes.

I hadn't meant to be in that part of town. I'd been helping a friend over in Bondi who'd fallen into trouble with a girl while visiting a certain establishment in Stanley Street. Hadn't seen the guy since high school but my name must have stuck. Or else it was the family connections to a range of quality recreational substances. Anyway, I did a bit of web poking for him. Reuters News delivers a nice stash of data on creatures great and small, from US presidents to nightclub 'hostesses' from Bexley. Ten minutes face to face were enough to send the troublesome lady back to the 'members lounge' of Azars (if they still had a job for her there). Stomping to the bus stop, she gave my mate the look from hell. Don't know why, when I was the one who'd sent her trotting. Pity. She was a forlorn kid, but not so young that pigtails suited her in broad daylight.

'I owe you one, mate,' he'd said. 'Suppose I could have sorted it, but two against one never hurts. By the way, how's the shop going in Rockdale? Your dad still doing those great chilli prawns?'

I was already checking my phone by then and missed most of it. He had a good memory. My dad still runs the local fish shop there. A frustrated chef, he insists on doing a Guangzhou menu on the side. The stink of deep-fried wontons wrapped up with chiko rolls has never left me.

The light rail to Uncle Hui's apartment in Bay Street crawled across George Street and through Chinatown. Uncle Hui was a hot-headed old bird who picked up strays every other week. This latest one had his stress ticker up to the limit – this was something sensitive.

Chinese tour groups were piling on for the casino as I got off. I used the time navigating the jam to brush up on my Cantonese but it wasn't going to impress old Uncle Hui – the words Harbour Bridge, Travelodge and Three Sisters weren't likely to crop up between us. I didn't want to hang around for tea and wontons, home-made or not. Old Hui would turn the talk around to family, which was old territory and whose complexities were beyond my Cantonese vocab. I planned to call in the reliable 'next meeting' to get me back out the front door before my shirt started creasing.

It had just gone four when I punched the intercom of the block and was answered by Hui's barked hello. He'd had his eye to the view hole. He cranked the door open so fast I thought I'd gone to a drug bust by mistake. But no, behind the opened door was Hui, slight and wiry as ever, and his even more slender missus, Nancy. She was shuffling from the living room to the kitchen in slippers with dirty plastic plates in her hands. A gnawed duck bone and a smear of hoisin sauce were the evidence of either a late lunch or her lazy housekeeping.

Hui had on his afternoon cream nylon shirt rolled to the elbow, black pants and plastic thongs. Nancy could have been mistaken for his daughter – the sulky one. The air was stale from the closed windows and mouldy armchairs, but it was probably better than the Western Distributor air roaring outside.

Hui let off a rattle of noise about how I hadn't changed and all those years of not showing my face to the family, and about my wasted police career and my destined decline via my business, run from a second-floor office in Liverpool Street. I just smiled and bowed. His barometer was high, judging by the way he grabbed at the limp hanky in his hand and ran it down his left leg like an addict with a skin rash. This latest forlorn dude was under his skin, so I decided to give him half an ear.

Between the front door and the brown lounge, he crammed in enough words to fill *War and Peace*, the Cantonese edition. A framed picture of Buddha gathered dust on the side table. As far as I knew, he'd never stepped into a temple in his life, unless it was to exchange cash with his Viet mate Van, his partner in a hotel laundry scam. Between them, they'd pocketed thousands over the years, most of it now swelling the pockets of James Packer's shareholders. He didn't know I knew, he and my dad both thought my Chinese was as good as Tony Abbott's. Shows how much time they spent talking to me between the prawn scallops and fish of the day at the shop.

The dude of the month was hunkered in the corner with his blotchy face glued to a rerun of *The Bachelor*. A sullen type, not too tall, not too short, not fat or thin. The crime division's photofit face from hell. While he thawed out, I flexed a few words on Nancy. A mess of a script I'd be embarrassed to use to an English speaker, but she appreciated it – it was probably the best conversation she'd had in weeks. Thirty years Hui's junior and he'd sponsored her from Shanghai a few years ago. It was no love match, but no doubt they both got something out of the arrangement.

The dude's name was Vinnie. He didn't seem to have a family name.

'A good boy, Vinnie's a good boy,' Hui insisted. 'Too many bad men out there, no trust. You five years with police. Safe there. Not now, you no there any more.' He grunted, a slap on the familiar if ever there was one. 'Now you must work long to get same place.'

'If Vinnie's a blushing rose, why is he hiding his bushel here in your flat?' The metaphors were a lingual car crash and perfectly pitched to annoy him.

He went ranting to Nancy, who'd taken her disappointed face to the cramped bedroom where she was reading the funnies in the *Chinese Daily*.

'You're in a cosy spot with Hui,' I said to Vinnie in English. If Hui didn't want to know about this business, I'd make it easier for him.

'Good man, all his family good men.' Vinnie slid an eye over me then back to *The Bachelor*. Clearly, I wasn't included in this fond crew.

'Must be a bad business to hole up with him like this,' I said. 'You want to share the joy? I've got a crock of work waiting for me back at the office.'

He sighed and I saw the muscles along his jaw ripple.

'I don't have a job.'

His English was pretty good for a ten-yearer. I guessed he'd come up under Howard. I also guessed Shanghai, but I'm no expert.

'Sorry, I don't do a pensioner discount.'

'I worked hard. Jobs hard to get even for cash. Not for you maybe, nice Aussie.'

I wasn't in the mood for envy.

'Job went sour on you. That it?'

'Job OK. Bankstown. I was doorman. Close to station and a clean place. All the girls Aussies, no Chinese. All legal.'

I saw it all right – one of those Indian sweet shop fronts running off from the bus interchange. The sign would say Taste of the Orient and would sell satay sauce in bottles and a stash of fresh herbs upfront. Ten metres in, there'd be stairs to the first floor, illuminated by the cheap in-step uplighting that passes for 'mood' in Wuhan. Five rooms upstairs, themed in pink, blue, red, green and gold. A de luxe suite for the local big guy at the back with a bar fridge stocked with everything from prosecco to Jamesons.

'Bet you made a bit in tips,' I said.

'Tips,' he grunted like Hui. They were clearly old pals. 'Think tips will fix this?' His right arm hung from his coat sleeve, pink and flaccid.

'Car accident?' I knew it wouldn't be, unless he was at fault and wanted to spin a deal with the other side.

'We get some mean men at club. Most OK, some…' He shook his head and eyeballed *The Bachelor*.

'You said it's a clean house, this joint.'

Nancy appeared with a tray of tea and crackers. I put away the cigarette I'd been flicking between my fingers since I'd walked in. Six months off the weed but I still liked holding one.

'Who know, eh? Who know what go on? The boss changed maybe two months ago. Old one gone, don't know, maybe go back to Taiwan. This new one, he come maybe two hours a week. Come, take the money I guess, go.'

'And you're left to hard word the joes, I get it.' It was getting humid and Vinnie was settling in for the full bio, so I tried to shift him along. 'So if it wasn't a car, what? And what do you want from me?'

'Most boys OK, no trouble. One day, a man I no see before try us. He a fussy guy, he not happy with service.'

'He rough up a girl?'

Vinnie shook his head. 'He complain, he make big noise. Money back. I say our house, I say it like the movies. You pay, maybe the movie not good, maybe you bored. You don't complain, you say hey, all movies different. All OK, you leave.'

'High art in your joint then?' I chuckled and sipped the tea. Hot and scented, I hadn't tasted that blend since I was a kid. Maybe it was nostalgia, maybe I was in the mood for a good yarn, but I let him go on.

'Boss policy, no refund, no favours – unless he say. So we work a deal, a new girl, a nice one too, Somalian. A bit of spice maybe cheer him up, eh?' His grin was a dentist's dream. He was starting to grate on me.

'So he got two for the price of one. Where does your arm come in?'

'He still not OK, but I not know. He left, no speak to me. I smile, I smile big, like he a big man…' He rubbed the wilted pink hand. It was shiny, it was like watching a butcher massage the pork sausages in his window. 'I finish twelve and he there waiting for me.'

'Out on the street?'

'In car park.'

'Alone?'

'One guy he watch from his car. He look like gorilla. Hair every-where, tattoos say they bad men.'

'Bikies?'

'Maybe. I don't know. He stink, his hair chest, dirty head, it stink while he bash me. What can I do? I come up to his shoulder, he punch and down I go…' Vinnie perched on the end of the couch and pointed some good fingers down to the floor.

'What did the cops do? Or didn't you call them?'

He shrugged and glanced in to where Hui and Nancy were playing cards. Hui opened the bedroom window and let in the peak hour rumble of cars and buses making a snail's pace west. I climbed out of the deep back-breaking couch and strolled across to pull the venetians on the long living room windows. It turned out the view was down past dust-encrusted air con units to the giant garbage bins which were shared by the hundred units. It was a canyon of soot, pigeon shit and peeling render.

'What did you have in mind?' If he was right, the chances of tracking the guy down seemed low. That's why I was there.

'My problem up here.' He pointed at his brain. 'Left hemiplegia, six weeks in hospital. After, still no good. I don't see good, I can't stand up long, I get weak.'

'What do the doctors say?'

'I need more than what Centrelink give me, how I drive now? I don't sleep good, I tired all the time…sometime I fall down. I need 40,000 dollars I work out, to get this better, pay bills. Maybe I never work again? What then?'

'I don't know what Hui said, but I'm not a life counsellor.' I was getting the idea now, I'd heard it before from my dad's pals years ago and from the guys warming the doorways down at the casinos. There were plenty of cash jobs around, but they came without the trimmings. I had my own problems by then, having quit the boys' club in Liverpool Street where my super and overtime were enough to keep life's demons at bay. Business was different, but I'd been lucky so far. 'Do your joes register?'

'No ID, just name and suburb.'

'False?'

'I search online, phone book, Telstra, library. No match.'

'He could be anywhere.'

'He know a man called Alex. I see them talk.'

'You got an address?'

Another shrug. He could weasel like the best. It was like watching a politician being blowtorched on the ABC.

It turned out this Alex was no more than a kid, some runner for one of the weed shops in Darlinghurst. But he'd been hanging around a property guy whose name was getting splashed in the society pages lately. This guy had got on the ladder doing some of the trades at Barangaroo. He'd moved onto a big eco tower in Rhodes. Now, word was he'd got his hands on half of Zetland. This big guy, called Zerko, had a share in Vinnie's shop and got a feed of loot monthly sent up to his space in Pacific Towers on Harris Street. He'd been known to splash it around, maybe 'cause he was still awash with it himself, being on the rise and still sweet on life. Whatever, this guy could be tweaked and might have a sniff of our leading man to boot. It took Vinnie twenty minutes and twelve commercial breaks to get all this out.

Hui was scowling from the saggy edge of his room-sized double bed, so I kicked it along a bit. I agreed to go with Vinnie and shake Zerko for loose change, but I wasn't making a federal case out of it. I figured two to three hours and a parking tab would do it. He grunted, which I took for a deal.

It was heavy going on Harris Street. It was summer and people with jobs, in uni or loafing it were heading out to mix it in Surry Hills or check out the ice cream parlours and cafés in Newtown. Cop cars were pulling over a Merc or two, probably hoping to score a bag of cannabis for off-duty appreciation.

The block used to be an adult education college. It had cleaned 1920s brick facias, a black granite floor and a glass elevator. It was the type of place where you paid an extra 1,000 a quarter for a car lift. Zerko was entertaining folks but let us in. Vinnie seemed to shrink at the door. He skulked behind me and cradled his bad arm as if he was carrying a Christmas ham.

They had three deep armchairs like you'd see in a gentlemen's club. A view across to the Anzac Bridge, a polished wooden floor that would make a racket to walk on. Against the strata rules, no doubt, but Zerko didn't seem the sensitive type.

'I know your face,' he said, looking at Vinnie. Zerko was slim with the pink linen shirt. He had hair styled to a cockerel's peak and after-shave you'd smell in Katoomba. His ruddy face told me he'd just come from the gym. Either that or he'd spent the last hour cleaning his oven.

'I'm Jack Wen,' I said. 'Vinnie brought me along for the company. Hope that's OK.'

'I get it.' He pointed vaguely our way, his eyes squinting with the effort of thought. 'Vinnie. I know you from… No, surely not from that joint.'

Vinnie started grinning with those Hollywood teeth while dragging his arm low like he'd just been handed a bag of cement. 'Ah, you re-member mate,' he said. 'We old friends right?'

'You look bad, mate. That arm. You catch it in a car door?'

'I unlucky, Zerko. At Jangos, with customer. You remember? You hear right?'

Zerko glanced at me, his eyes narrowing. 'A bad nut.'

'Right.'

'I heard that Gazetti mob were bad news.' He walked over to tower over Vinnie. His chair hissed with relief. 'So where do I come in? Vin-nie?' He had a weary half-inebriated smile.

His mates munched on corn chips which spilt from a glass bowl. A big night ahead.

'I'm on last dollars, Zerko. No more job at Jangos.'

'What? Talk to Milko. He's the boss.'

Vinnie spilt the whole saga again with feeling. His cheeks were blotching to a nasty rash.

'Some crowbar job.' Zerko started patting his shoulder. 'Let me see it, Vinnie. Milko mentioned it. He didn't say how bad, though.'

Vinnie went pale and seemed to pull back. The other two birds had stayed on their perch. I thought it odd Zerko hadn't asked them to leave.

'Zerko, you know me. You see me…see this.'

'I do, man. You think I'm blind?'

He turned to me, leaned deep into my face and I was hit by a cyclonic cocktail of beer and Urban Jungle or whatever it was.

'Small business is dangerous, Jack.'

'Tell me about it.' I half laughed. 'I owe the tax office for the first time in my life.'

'I mean real danger, Jack.' He'd gone serious. He was a preacher in the making. 'This happens to a guy, a couple of mafia heavies decide to lean on him…things go bad, and then what?'

'Yeah?' Something was itching behind my brain but it hadn't made it to the surface yet. 'Vinnie thinks you know the deal with Jangos. Vinnie says you're a mate with a conscience.'

'I'm a small businessman, Jack. I'm up to my neck in debt. I'm sure you understand.'

Vinnie started to yabber again, acrid stuff bubbling from some bitter depth about his physio and the nurses and the guy at Centrelink who'd sent him on his way. He'd set the depth of his beady eyes on Zerko. Not a charm offensive by any means.

I butt in before he really soured the pie. 'Can you see your way to helping us out here, Zerko? We're not talking a lot.'

'Depends on what you mean, doesn't it? Those stamp duties bastards have bled me dry.'

'The hard life of a businessman, eh?'

'Stay off the pedestal, mate. Bucks don't breed like rabbits, I need every 40K in the can to stay afloat.'

'You look like you can afford it, mate – not a bad office you got here, Zerko. I presume it's yours?' He had some equity somewhere.

The two birds liked my question, one chortled till his gut wobbled, the other one leaned back in his chair as if waiting for the main show – whatever that was – to get going. He didn't have long to wait.

'Look, Vinnie.' Zerko opened his palms. 'Milko tells me he's got State Revenue breathing down his neck. If this joe is the creep I hear he is, there's gotta be a way to get some action.'

Vinnie muttered something in Cantonese, I didn't understand it but it wasn't polite.

'No good, Zerko,' he said at last. 'No cops.'

'Not too late from what I hear. I'll stand by you. I hear you're a good boy. Give me the cop's incident number and I'll ask around.'

'If you know this guy Gazetti, we're on easy street,' I said.

'Well, maybe it was him…' Zerko scratched behind his ear and frowned.

The mates in their chairs had stopped chomping and Vinnie was swaying from side to side. That itching in my brain got loud.

'Funny how you mentioned 40K just now.' There was a cigarette in my hand, I don't know how it got there. 'The figure Vinnie gave me before was the same. You a clairvoyant or something, Zerko?'

He laughed and I got a glistening view of his wide upper palate. The others were still. Even Vinnie seemed to be frozen to a spot on the floorboards. Beads of sweat were dripping from the end of his paralysed fingers.

I felt a chill creep round my shoulders. We were twenty floors up, the door was at least five metres away, I couldn't remember where the fire escape had been. It was too late. There was an initial wash of pain round my temple, then the blanket of nausea, and then nothing.

My neck was twisted painfully, I was moving, or should I say the car was, taking me to some slime pit beside the fish market, where Zerko must have a room to spare for dirty jobs. The back seat floor stank of rubber and cleaning fluid – there'd been action in that cramped corner before. Craning up, I saw Vinnie. The weasel was slumped away from me, peering down at me like I had AIDS or was going to bleed on him. The car turned a corner, I fought the instinct to vomit. Moving my right hand, I got pins and needles and a shaft of pain across my back. Maybe the lights would be lucky, maybe not. I took some breaths, pushed the pain away like they'd taught me in the cops. We were near the Star. I saw the logo leering at a crazy angle, saw the Lyric Theatre's latest show in lights. I wouldn't get a better chance than this.

The car slowed. A quiet machine, had to be a BMW sports. I reached up and crunched Vinnie's balls hard as I could and felt the little sack wriggle. He squealed and thrashed like a kid being dragged down the aisle of a supermarket. The car stopped.

'Open the door or I'll cripple you,' I growled.

His good hand shot to the door, it was a matter of seconds. We tumbled out into the glare of the post theatre crowd. He was crying like a baby, wailing in a mixture of Cantonese and English. I was out of there and pushing up the footpath, up the huge set of stairs and into the crowd. I could hear running behind me and a woman swearing. They'd taken out a stroller and kids and the mountain man husband was using some fists. I thanked God for matinee family deals.

It was a couple of hours before I lost them. It was midnight when I stumbled into my office on Liverpool Street. The security guy, Len, nodded and kept to himself. He was a shrewd man.

Inside, I took a slug from the Jack Daniels I kept under my desk. I'm not much of a drinker, but I make the odd exception.

Tapping it into my laptop made me feel better. It started to gel and come to life. By dawn, I had it ready to email to my mate Col across the road in the fraud squad. But there was no hurry. I was manky as hell but Coletto's across the road fed coffee to barristers or junkies, they didn't care. As I finished my bacon and egg roll, I decided I'd let Vinnie have a chance. Maybe I was feeling saintly, maybe just lucky.

I tracked him down from Hui. The old man couldn't look me in the eye.

'Should have known better, uncle,' I said.

He scowled but for once didn't crank up the diatribe. My bruised neck was a reprimand.

Vinnie was sitting back row of a funeral in St Lawrence's Church on Broadway for some old Greek woman he didn't know. He fanned himself with the coloured program featuring lavender fronds and cute pics of the old girl as a kid. I wondered what they'd put on my program when the day came. Vinnie had a clean shirt and combed hair. Someone loved him then. But I was betting it wouldn't be our mutual friend Zerko.

'This church doesn't stay open for ever. Where then, Vinnie?'

He just huffed, fanned himself, pretended to listen to the white-haired priest with the pretty green gown up front. He was a puny dog, except dogs are loyal. A desperate ferret, like the type that get hunted to near extinction in some old movie set in the jungle. Only no one would bother getting a sweat hunting this runt down. OK, so he had a limp arm, poor guy. Somehow I didn't care.

'I want Zerko called off – right, Vinnie?'

'Zerko, he a mad man.'

'You cranked him up, Vinnie. You and who – your boss?'

'Jack, you make me laugh.' He didn't break a smile.

'You wanted the 40K all right, didn't you, but not for this thing.' I flicked at the arm. It was dry for once. He'd discovered talcum powder. 'You got a bit owing, haven't you? Maybe to Zerko, maybe some other mob, I don't know. I bet Zerko's friends worked you over too, and you'd agreed on a story. But dumb old Zerko spilt the beans. I thought it was funny he mentioned the exact amount you needed, 40K, which happens to be exactly what the court will cough up for a criminal compensation payout. He was in on it. Helping the show along, so to speak.' It was a guess, but his furtive glances at the floor told me I'd guessed right. Vinnie was a gambler who'd gone a round too many and owed the wrong sort of guy. 'But you couldn't pay it. So they pointed you to the proceeds of crime unit.'

It was an old scam, so how had I missed it? A guy can't pay, his kindly creditors help him out by doing him over for free, leaving him with a tidy victims comp claim for 40K for the beat-up from some faceless crook.

'But the department wasn't biting, right?' I had to whisper – the brother was doing his eulogy up front.

A couple of men in nice suits had turned and were frowning at us.

'So you needed me to beef it up a bit. They know me over there, the boys in blue. You figured I'd help the tale along.'

'They never paid me right at Jangos. I needed money. What I do?'

'Someone else's always to blame, right?'

He was easy to shift from the pew. We shuffled out of the funeral like the grieving relations we were. On George Street, it was muggy and the neon lights were unnaturally lurid under a heavy sky. I wanted the rain, I wanted it to wash Vinnie's antiseptic talc odour from me.

He showed me the joint he was holed up in. A room over the Malaya House on Bathurst Street. I'm not the malicious type so I nutted out an olive branch for him to scramble up onto.

'You could go down for attempted fraud, Vinnie, and I know a few of the sweet chaps who could do with a good conviction on their sheets.'

He waited, pulling a greasy teacup from a shelf over his microwave. He opened a window to let in air and a gust of damp air sent packets of instant noodles tumbling to the floor.

'You tell me, Jackie.' He was hardening up – a good sign. I could chalk my name on him now.

'I know a guy over in Redfern who runs a nice place. He needs a Mandarin speaker for the phone. No cash handling. A nice easy job. Should cover your rent here. I'll help you cut a deal to pay off what you owe. In return, you can have a chat with Zerko, explain the misunderstanding we had.'

'That it, Jackie?'

'We'll stay friends and I'll pop by now and then, just to see how you're going. And chat. Sound OK?'

His face sagged to match his arm, but he could nod well enough.

We had a deal. Thunder rippled along the mean laneway outside. He lit a cigarette. I let him suck the smoke and watched the heavy drops splash against the rusting window frame. Wind pushed sheets of it through the window where it dumped onto the peeling linoleum on the benches. Vinnie didn't move.

Leaving the flat, I made a mental note of a possible day next month to pop by and hear his gossip. Then the next month and the one after that. He was a start-up, you might say. He might fail on me, but he might fly. I pulled my collar close but the rain drenched my clothes and flooded my shoes.

Chinatown was awash with umbrellas and flooded gutters. Soaked tourists were huddling in the doorways of fogged up barbecue houses and running between cars in ragged pairs. Staff in the import shops selling jade and bamboo toys and satin dolls put tea towels along their doorways. It was days like that I thought of the old folks and the mates in Goulburn Street and the girls I'd moved on from. Call me a sentimental type, strolling wet streets like some B-grade cop who'd just thrown in his badge. I'd let little Vinnie and his pink arm get to me.

I wanted cleansed of his tiny flat, so I kept walking while a Dreamliner groaned overhead through the storm. I hit a corner and found myself opposite the Belvedere on Kent Street. It was open – when aren't pubs open these days? Water was cascading off the deep veranda and into the drains. I stepped in and found a sodden cigarette in my hands. The air con was arctic. Wet to the bone, I'd be lucky if I didn't get pneumonia. The bar tender poured me a whisky. I waited for night to fall.

4

Auburn

Bronwyn turned up her podcast to block out the noise of the kids. The train was crowded for late morning. Why weren't those little creeps at school? Pants hanging below their arses, leaking drink cups, their bags dragging over the gritty floor of the train.

The train flashed through the mess of the inner west – ageing office towers, cheap apartment blocks and tiny terraces crammed against each other. The train slowed at Auburn station and as the doors opened, the strollers and packs of sullen kids shoved past her.

'For Chrisssake,' she muttered. She didn't want a scene, she believed in avoiding confrontation wherever possible.

Daisy would have bought pies from one of these grease pits lining the tawdry shopping strip. Knowing she should contribute something, Bronwyn popped into a Vietnamese bakery and bought a few custard tarts.

Climbing Auburn Road, she passed a hairdresser with an old Arab smoking out front. She was sure he'd blow smoke in her face, so she hurried on. Nothing escaped the wide mirrors inside the shop. She hadn't seen one like that since she was a kid and they went as a family on Saturday mornings to the Greek man down the road. He'd worked out of the back room of his fibro house and had a Maltese terrier called Pip which drooled at your feet.

Her stockings itched where the sun hit her legs. They were new shoes. She wanted to look good for old Daisy.

Behind the shopping mall, a council van was parked with a pair of guys inside having their lunch. So far, they were the only white people she'd seen. Baklava was displayed neatly under the counter of one of the cafés, and further into the shop a tube of meat had started to sizzle on a spit. A boy with a weedy beard smiled at her and indicated the sweets. She turned away but all she could see was the other side of the road and the Centrelink office with its orange logo gleaming under the dull sky.

She wanted a coffee but wouldn't sit next to the men who were spilling cigarette soot onto the footpath. She'd given up smokes years ago, but every day she woke with the old hunger. Daisy's post-lunch tea would have to do. A weekday out in the world was strange to her. When on holidays, it'd always been Bali, or Surfers or, back in her forties, France with the girls from the club. When not on holidays, the office. This morning she'd dressed by rote – the stockings, the ironed white shirt, the grey skirt, the black jacket.

A sign announced the new council chambers, the library and the civic square. She saw a cavernous monolith funded by municipal money. An old couple sat in the gloomy concourse with a shopping trolley, tearing apart a bun. Her father had worked in the old council building. She'd gone to functions as a girl and served egg and lettuce sandwiches on a tray, carrying it around the musty chamber which had smelt of timber polish.

The library used to be made of red bricks with row upon row of books. She used to sit cross-legged among the aisles on Friday afternoons looking through *National Geographic*. Foreign places were foreign then. Peering inside, she couldn't see a single book, but there were plenty of brightly coloured beanbags and a row of PCs.

The stretch to Daisy's house seemed long. As a child, nothing seemed long, the humid walks from school, the languid teenage hours waiting for boys at the milk bar where the Migrant Education Centre now stood. The milk bar had been a west facing hot place, the milk in the icy metal tubs gorgeous relief against your palms. There were the afternoons spent waiting for Danny, the lies she'd told her mother, the angry sidewards glances she received arriving home.

'You'll not do that again, girl, or you'll have your ears whacked.'

Her mother's constant admonitions mingled with the talkback radio. Sausages frying in the sweltering kitchen, they'd eat when her father got home at God knew what hour. How she'd hated those gnarled lumps. Danny took an apprenticeship with an air conditioning repairer, and within two years was in Texas working for some multinational. There'd been a letter or two between them, then nothing. He'd made some mention about her going out there too, but she knew he didn't mean it.

Daisy was on the veranda watering pot plants.

'I'm not late, am I?' Bronwyn called up as she mounted the cracked front steps.

'What does it matter anyway?' answered Daisy, smiling. This was true. Daisy was scrawny, her thinned grey hair cropped short, her back slightly stooped. God, she used to be so elegant, the one who looked good in a bikini.

The lawn was pale, hard, you could play tennis on it. She remembered the first time they'd met at a netball game in Lidcombe, a Saturday morning with a storm brewing up from the west. Daisy scribbling in her puzzle book at the break, orange juice drying acid in her fingernails. She'd said she could finish a book a week, had piles of finished ones on her bedroom dresser. An easy person to buy Christmas presents for, they'd always laughed.

They walked down the dark hall to the small kitchen at the back of the house. A modern double storey loomed from the house behind casting shadows over the backyard. She glimpsed the flapping of Indian garments on the clothes line next door. Deep reds, browns, a thin strip of gold catching the sun.

'It's warming up already,' said Daisy.

'I picked up some sweets for afters. I hope they're all right.'

'Hmm, sweets always welcome.' Daisy took it with a weak smile and slipped it onto the kitchen bench. 'Sorry about the mess,' she said, shifting plastic bags stuffed with clothes. 'I didn't get around to any of this while Dad was alive.'

'That's understandable. You're thinking of moving?'

'Where would I go?' Shedding her jacket, Bronwyn glanced around the place.

The kitchen hadn't been renovated, Daisy's dad had always been stingy. An odour of lamb fat drifted from the frypan soaking in the sink. Looking at Daisy's thin skirt and bare feet, Bronwyn realised she was overdressed. Daisy had cared for her dad at home till the end. The parent's bedroom had looked like a hospital – the hydraulic bed, the wheelchair under the window, the pills so organised in the pharmacy pack. Daisy as cheerful as ever, she'd taken to sudoku and could get through five a day with no trouble, sitting in the rocker a metre from the bed.

She didn't know why she hadn't visited Daisy in the last months – she'd had no idea how bad it had become. She'd used work as an excuse. Her firm, Bridges, had been understaffed and she'd stayed back many a night sorting out the accounts. It'd been manageable. She'd been proud of the clearance rate she'd achieved. No surprises there, Brett had said, you could run this place with one hand tied behind your back. Words to spur her on. She'd surpassed herself refining the estimate for the tax deadline, worked out the redundancies for the ones who'd gone, had talked over the revised plans for the Asian campaign with Brett over those coffees. Brett had paid most days, had occasionally come back from the counter with a stash of chocolate bars for her.

Daisy removed a tottering pile of old bills and bank statements and dumped them on the floor in a corner behind the couch. The stench of cigarettes clung to the place despite the fact that no one had smoked there for years. It was still fresh for Bronwyn – Saturday afternoon with Daisy's father reading the racing guide, a cigarette tray balanced on the edge of the sofa, she and Daisy playing Monopoly on the brown shag pile.

'Now, let's get those photos out,' Daisy said. She reached into an overstuffed drawer.

'Not in albums then?' Bronwyn asked, eyeing the old ring binders in the bookcase.

'These weren't good enough to keep, really. Just…scraps really.'

But good enough to offer to her old friend. She suppressed this mean reflection.

Flicking through the photos, she felt herself growing impatient. This was trash she'd have dumped twenty years ago – blurred shots of them running up a netball court, row after row of kids' faces in classroom portraits, a girl she could barely remember standing on a veranda of a bush hut on some camp. From memory, they'd spent that bored, rain-filled weekend squashing snails on a damp veranda.

At the office, she'd have stopped after ten minutes, said, 'OK, so the point of this is?' in the flippant but restrained way she'd honed. A career's work, the navigation of tough relationships, the excitement when she'd clinched a big deal, the tedium of grinding through the office politics. Twenty years at Bridges, her diary always crammed with appointments and the names of key contacts. From today, the pages blank – what did any of that matter now?

'What time is it?' She hoped it didn't come out as rude.

'Oh yes, let's look at some lunch,' said Daisy.

'So did he appreciate you at the end do you think? Your dad?'

'That's out of nowhere.'

Bronwyn noticed the front door was still open. 'Shouldn't you lock that?' she asked.

'It's a nice breeze.'

A car revved past out front, sending up a pool of exhaust. Some fresh air.

'Oh, look at that,' said Daisy. 'Oh, my God!'

Polaroids were stuck together and Daisy pulled them apart, tearing the corners. Taken of each other in the front yard using the new camera, such a novelty, the photos spitting out immediately and falling on the grass in front of them. Sunlight bleaching the shots, sky too blue to be real, their dresses lurid gold, a colour in fashion at the time.

Bronwyn rose and reached for her mobile. Nothing there. No Brett, none of the girls.

Daisy got the plates down and, reaching into the fridge, produced a plate of sandwiches – tuna, mayonnaise and salad.

'So what happened with all that trouble at your work?'

'Oh, that's all over now.'

'Must be a relief.'

That was one way to describe it. Like the quiet pill, the type given to dogs. Strolling to the kitchen, she wanted to drop her shoes off, patter in bare feet behind Daisy. But how to do it, how to shed that skin which had been hers for so long?

In the kitchen, Daisy fiddled with the sandwiches, rummaged in cupboards as if unable to find the right utensils. At the back of the cupboards, the old wallpaper was still there, the floral green, bubbling slightly.

Daisy tugged some paper napkins from a drawer crammed with what looked like salvage from every coffee shop she'd ever been to – napkins, sugar sachets, plastic spoons. 'It's been ages since we did this,' she said.

'Did we ever?'

'Well, you know.'

'Nice to be back on old turf, that's for sure.'

'You know the leagues club's being sold for flats?' Daisy's eyes were pained.

'Oh, really?' Bronwyn wasn't going to pretend she cared. It had always been a dump. 'Well, that's Sydney for you, always changing. You should come into town more. Jesus, the whole place is a construction site.'

'But the club – I'm glad Dad didn't live to see it.'

'He wasn't a member, was he?'

'It doesn't matter.'

'Everything moves on, Daisy.'

'Not everything.'

'Oh, yes. Think of me, last week.' Bronwyn tucked her new photos away. 'I'd never dreamt of quitting.'

'You don't regret it?'

'What's to regret? It was time.'

The tarts were still on the stove top. Daisy started to take the glad wrap off the sandwiches.

'Oh, a visitor.' Daisy's voice suddenly became light and breathy.

There were footsteps at the back door and a man, an Indian, appeared holding a saucer with a sliced-up grapefruit on it.

'Oh, Sanit!' said Daisy.

He stepped in, leaving his shoes on the low cement step. A quiet smile at Bronwyn, a nod of the head. He had huge dark eyes which seemed to laugh at her.

Daisy was suddenly busy with the kettle and the plates. Smiling, she took the saucer. 'Oh, that looks wonderful. Bronwyn, this is my neighbour, Sanit. He has a way with fruit, just look at this.'

It was grapefruit, what was there to say about it? Bronwyn hadn't expected this guy. How did he get into the backyard anyway?

'Bronwyn's been helping me with some of Dad's stuff.'

Had she?

'Ahh,' said Sanit. 'Lots to do. You keeping little Daisy on her toes.'

'I'll take as much help as I can get!'

'He was an old man, we all get old. It is best.' Sanit sat down at one of the kitchen tables, uninvited.

'It certainly leaves me more time on my hands.'

'Maybe too much.' Bronwyn guffawed and slurped at the tea Daisy handed her. It was too hot and she scalded her tongue. 'Oh, fuck!'

'Bronwyn, mind!' Daisy exclaimed as if she'd never heard the word.

'Oh, don't be a prude, Daisy!'

'Tea for you, Sanit?' Daisy had blushed slightly.

'Come, Bronwyn love, sit down. Daisy makes a lovely brew.' It was Sanit asking, waving his slim brown arm at her.

Bronwyn felt a a small fury at the man's words. At Bridges, she'd have taken this man aside and spoken to him. If truth be said, this man would not have been at Bridges in the first place. Her last day had been

Wednesday. Two days of weekday that followed, the abyss of the weeks to follow. She'd slammed the door as she'd left.

'You visit Daisy often for tea, Sanit?'

'It is excellent company here.'

'That's not what I asked.'

Daisy turned her head sharply. 'Bronwyn!'

'I was just asking.'

'No, you weren't.'

'What?'

'Ladies,' Sanit interrupted, moving sandwiches onto plates. 'Come, it is warm out, let us cool down and enjoy this delicious meal.'

'This tea makes me hot. Daisy looks hot too.'

'Don't speak for me.'

'Tea cools the blood,' said Sanit. 'Always good for hot days. And Daisy makes a good pot.'

'You know a lot about Daisy. She's a hard worker, bet you've worked that out.'

'Oh yes, I know.' He nodded in admiration.

'She worked for her dad like a slave for twenty years. She's had enough of all that.'

Daisy took a loud intake of breath and brought her hand to her mouth. 'What's got into you?'

Bronwyn slammed down her teacup into the white saucer. She thought of the brilliant white blouses she wore in her early days, fresh from business college. Just as cheap and mediocre.

Daisy offered her a sandwich but she refused, and then one of the tarts. She said she was on a diet and passed that up too. She ran over the train timetable in her head, the wait on the platform amidst the teeming masses of multicultural Sydney. It'd be nearly two by the time she got into the city. And then what? She had been flung from the arms of the clock. Time spun on railway platforms, in offices, on mobiles, leaving her behind. She muttered some words about a meeting and grabbed her bag.

Descending the steps, she noticed the property opposite had become a mess of broken earth and brick slabs. One day, that'd be Daisy's house, gone and replaced with 'dwellings' squeezed into the tight boundary. She'd never gone back to her old house to see what the developers had done to it.

'Bron, hey, what is this?' Daisy was huffing behind her down the stairs. 'Where are you going? Don't be stupid.'

Bronwyn rounded to stare up at her. 'You've got to get out of here, out of this mess.' Venom spilt from her voice.

'What mess?'

She sighed, and fingered the straps of her bag. 'That man. He's not for you.'

'You don't know him. Maybe…maybe you don't know me. Bronwyn, what's got into you?'

'He's just going to exploit you. He wants a maid.'

'You don't like him 'cause he's Indian. That's it, isn't it?'

Bronwyn turned round and marched, head down, to the rusted front fence.

'You're bitter, Bronwyn. You're…they sacked you, didn't they?'

Bronwyn grabbed the gate – its exposed iron scorched her hand.

'You said to move on.' Daisy was yelling, determined to be heard. She had the voice of an old harpy bleating to herself at a bus shelter.

Bronwyn thought of that man, Sanit. Daisy would go back inside and drink tea with him, they'd see each other again tomorrow, that side gate would open and close, the days would pass in the sticky Auburn heat. Daisy wouldn't die alone. Without looking back, she slammed the gate and started walking.

It was eleven thirty by her mobile, and by now Ahmed would be working on her projections. At four, Brett would take him to the café. If she hurried, she could be in town and there by one thirty. She and Brett had had spats before. Who didn't? That was business. They went back a long way, he still had a lot to learn. She started to rehearse her opening words. 'Mate, look, about last week, let's go out and talk…'

Wandering along the dilapidated shopping strip, the past swarmed into her head. The summer afternoons buying ice blocks from the corner store, still there and still selling lollies in small cardboard boxes. But it also sold long pale green vegetables she didn't know in large boxes from the market, nuts in plastic trays, bananas. She went inside and stalked the dark hot aisles. Behind the counter a Pacific Islander man was drinking a pale red tea.

Down in the main street, she went into the café where the old men had been earlier. It was getting to lunchtime and young office workers queued to buy kebabs and chips, women loaded with shopping stood blocking the passageway with silverbeet protruding from their trolleys. Taking an outside table to get a coffee and a piece of baklava, she felt humid air sweeping in from the road and the steaming wheels of the cars. By one o'clock, she was still there. A flabby-armed woman in a Turkish head scarf called her luv and asked her if she was all right. The woman looked concerned, and she realised her own face was flushed and clammy. The coffee had left her mouth parched. A storm was building, she could see the clouds swirling in the reflective awning of the bank opposite. A chill breeze was sweeping down the hill where the open Auburn streets lay exposed under the sky.

Her jacket was damp, she smelt herself on it. Tearing it off, she shoved it in the ash-smeared garbage bin outside the café. She walked. Round the block, down past the shopping centre car park where the cars beeped her, into the library where she fingered the novels and magazines. The place smelt like school, and she tried to trace the years since she'd studied in these places, had written homework and made plans for some adult life away from these dreary few miles of Sydney.

Exiting the automatic doors, she saw that time had passed. People were picking up kids and café owners were sweeping the pavements. When the rain came, she didn't seek cover, she let it flood her stockings, the leather of her shoes, the delicate skin at the base of her ear, which she hadn't touched for years. Walking, she diverted back down the lane, past the mall and the plastic-shrouded prams and the takeaway wrappers which tumbled down the draughty road.

A voice called softly. She turned.

It was the old Turkish woman, holding the bedraggled jacket she'd abandoned hours ago. The woman had wrapped it in a tea towel and put it in a plastic bag. 'You OK, luv?' she asked again. The woman was puffing slightly, she must have spotted her and hurried to catch her up.

Bronwyn took the bag and looked into the woman's old grey eyes. From somewhere she found a weak, mechanical smile, but it was enough.

At the train station, the timetable was all wrong. Gone was the twelve fifty-two she'd catch to town for the movies with Daisy, the six twenty-eight with Danny to the rambling nights in city pubs with his mates, the last one home, the twelve forty-two from Central, arriving home one twenty-three. Grabbing her phone, she looked up the new times. Rainwater, trapped on the curve of her eyelid, cooled her whole head. The Turkish woman had been kind. She would never have bothered doing that for a stranger. She tipped the jacket into a railway bin, and immediately felt lighter and less encumbered.

Walking back up the station stairs, she returned to the streets. At the zebra crossing, a group of boys was tumbling past. Rainwater evaporated from the road. Thunder was rolling in again. She was sodden, and the next dumping was heading towards Auburn. But she knew Daisy would lend her something dry.

5

Toongabbie

There was a rifle under the house. I sniffed it and it reeked of oil and blankets. Lesley was the first to touch it – she's the shortest, so it was easier for her to creep under the house and drag out all the rusted chairs and the suitcases, the dirt-caked bottles and all the broken dolls we'd thrown there as kids. And the rifle.

Lesley didn't seem to mind touching it. Made we wonder at the time, and I wonder how much I really know now. All three of us were there – my brother Nathan, Lesley my sister, and me.

There was a bit of rusted wire fencing down there from where the chooks used to be kept, part of Mum's plan to make us self-sufficient, like we used to be out at Walgett before we moved to Toongabbie. Lasted about a week before every poor chook was eaten by the feral cats. Mum couldn't make a fence to save herself. Dad didn't want chooks, said they smelt bad, wanted proper eggs from the shops. Neither of them that smart, to tell the truth, and remembering Lesley creeping out holding that gun, I guess it's hereditary. She caught the rifle in the wire coming out and slipped in the dust, sending up a cloud. As it passed my face, I gulped in Christ knows what kind of crap. I couldn't fool myself from then on as to who'd owned it. On those few nights Dad had come home in a good mood, and full of cuddles, he'd smelt like that.

'Oh, my lord,' said Nathan.

'A whopper,' answered Lesley, with a sly grin. 'A big bloody whopper.'

'Oh, dear lord.'

'A heavy bastard, a real grown-ups' toy, fuck.'

'All right!' I said. They'd made the point. 'Where the hell did that come from? And Lesley, can you please drop it?'

'Don't think so, Sandra,' she smirked. And, sure enough, she carefully placed it on the grass as if she knew what she was doing.

The paper bag Nathan had brought his lunch in blew past and dumped an inch of tomato sauce on it.

Lesley rubbed it off with the hem of her torn jeans. 'No rushing with this baby. It'll go off.'

'If it's got bullets.'

'It might.'

'Hmm, maybe.'

'Oh, fuck – a gun.' Nathan was sweating. He didn't get out much these days between the days at the bank, the three kids and the church, which seemed to be eating him up. 'This is kind of…'

'Unbelievable.'

My voice was obliterated by the tremor of a goods train thumping past. The house was wedged in the triangle between the cement works, the train station and public school. The fibro houses were still scattered around the bare streets, but one by one, the grasses were rising in the lawns, the houses shrinking between the scorched earth of development. Our house would be no different.

The sun was creeping west. You could still see the horizon in that street, it had been vegetable-growing land once, and a few farm weatherboard cottages dotted the back streets. In winter, chill mountain driven air had leeched through the thin walls of our home. It'd been a few years since I'd been to Toongabbie. But parents will die and I couldn't leave Lesley and Nathan to sort it all out alone. The rifle was heavy in the knotted grass. Mum liked to keep that lawn mowed to within an inch of its life and walking on it was like stepping across a hessian rug.

'So what do we do?' I asked.

'Geeze, it's a bit difficult,' answered Lesley.

'My lord,' moaned Nathan. 'Cathy won't like this.' His wife didn't like much as it was.

Lesley threw off her baseball cap and pushed at her wet fringe. She was skinny and that long hair didn't suit her. 'Oh, for God's sake, Nathan,' she said. 'Cathy doesn't need to know, does she?'

'What a thing…'

'It's fine. All right? It's just a gun. There's hundreds of them around.'

'Shh,' I said. 'Not so loud.' We didn't know these new neighbours.

Nathan staggered over to the carport and slumped in the old armchair with the cigarette burn marks on the arms. It would have been hot under that tin roof. Cathy always ironed his clothes but the cotton shirt he had on was creased and damp across the chest. Only Nathan would wear a shirt like that for work like this. Mum had died only a month before. Buried next to Dad now, out at Kemps Creek cemetery under a parched stretch of earth dotted with wilting flowers. So it was just the house, which was pretty well done. Despite the council ban, Lesley had insisted on a bonfire to get rid of the decade's worth of *Woman's Day* magazines. Said she didn't want to pay the tip fees, but really it was an excuse for a street party. You'd think the smog from summer hazard reduction would have been enough for them, but they all turned up, the old crowd from the club and the church and the barbecue nights of old, beaming at the sight of an illegal blaze. As he left, the widower from two doors up, with a formal sort of bow, thanked us for inviting him.

'Look,' I said to Lesley as we eyed the gun. 'Nathan doesn't want much to do with this. Cathy'll just make a fuss. Why don't we just… Put that thing back and forget about it. For the time being anyway.'

'It's not gonna go away, you know.' She was rubbing her index finger along it. 'We can't just pretend we didn't find it.'

'I'm not saying ignore it. Just leave it for today – it's after five. We've got the rest of the junk to deal with.'

'Didn't you just say Nathan was finished? So let's leave the rest.'

'Yeah. And the rifle.'

She sat down next to it and rested her hand on the smooth wood of the handle. Sweat seeped into my armpits.

'What's with you and that thing, Lesley? Touching it.'

'It's nothing,' she said. 'Come on, have a feel.' Lying back, she petted the grey shaft.

'I don't want a feel,' I said, suddenly sick of the sight of her.

I walked across to Nathan. He was answering a text from one of the kids who, as usual, wanted to be picked up from some soccer match. He spent his life driving those kids around or doing free jobs for the church like mowing the lawn and painting the function hall.

'You heading off, Nath?' I asked.

'Paulie needs a lift from soccer.'

'I've had enough here.'

'Are we calling the police? You know, about that?' He looked at the rifle. 'I don't like it.'

He was right, we should go to the police. But they wouldn't just take it off our hands and say thank you very much. They'd want answers. Bloody Dad: even when we were kids, he was always making a mess – a bruised cheek, a TAB bill, the dregs of a can of beer on the kitchen floor. Even dead, he was causing grief.

'Lesley,' I asked, 'will you take it to the cops?'

'Not today. Later maybe.' Lesley had rested the rifle against the garage door and was shaking the blanket. A plume of dust rose in the hazy sky. Then she hung the blanket over the old clothes line.

'What's Lesley doing?' Nathan asked.

'Getting dirty,' I answered.

We left her to it. When I got to the house the next morning nothing had changed. There was the same pile of junk from under the house stacked up against the back fence – roof tiles in a collapsing cardboard box, the broken washing machine, a smashed wardrobe door.

Lesley was sifting through it. 'This brings back memories,' she said.

It was hard to believe this rubble had once been part of our lives. I don't know what Lesley was remembering at that moment. She was short, like our mother, and had our mother's thin frame. They'd both been easy for Dad to work over.

'I can feel another bonfire coming on,' I said.

We both laughed. I was glad Nathan hadn't come back. Something had come up with one of the kids. He would've been something else to worry about. The day was a cooler one. Rain was spitting against the leaves of the wattle tree in the back yard. That was the only thing from the block worth saving.

'I've boiled the kettle,' said Lesley. 'Let's go inside.' She'd set up some cups, a pack of biscuits, a tea towel. She'd made it almost cosy. 'Look, about that rifle. We need to talk.'

'Yeah?' I was glad she'd mentioned it first.

'I've got a mate who can help us.'

'Oh, right?'

'Yeah, get rid of it for us. You know…so there's no trouble, no has-sle.'

'Oh, right, what do you have in mind?' Did she know some guy in the police?

The tea she handed me was milky and sweet. It was the same brand Mum had used, the very same tea in fact.

'It's going to be bloody awkward.' She half laughed.

'I'll say. But if you can do something…fabulous.'

'Of course. It'll be a pain.'

'Look, Dad went off lots – who knows? I mean…'

'If he used it?'

Turning round to put her cup down, she spilt the tea. A cloudy pool formed on the laminate and soaked through an inch of exposed particle board. The whole place needed demolishing.

'Who knows?' she said.

'It's possible.'

'Which makes it even more important that we don't go to the police about it.'

'Huh?' I blinked at her. 'Not hand it in, you mean?'

'Dad might have done stuff. Who knows.'

'But he's dead now.'

'He still has a name. Still has a…honour.'

Did he ever?

'You planning to bury it then? Out at Walgett somewhere? Back out there? You can't keep it round here. It's gotta die, Lesley – like him.'

'My mate thinks it's a bad idea to hand it in. And I trust him.' Her jaw was set hard.

'Why? And who the hell is this friend anyway?'

'I didn't say friend.'

'What then?'

'A mate. That's all.'

Steady rain had started outside. The sweet smell of wet earth drifted in through the back door. If you demolished that house, you could make a decent garden, grow vegetables like in the old days, plant another tree or two. But I couldn't see the yard now without the rifle.

'Lesley,' I said. 'I don't know. Isn't it illegal or something?'

She snorted. 'If you trust the cops, you're an idiot.'

'Come on,' I said, fed up with her. 'Let's go and do it right now. It's our gun, right?' I wasn't going to shift. I'd felt sorry for her for as long as I could remember and had always given in. But how long does that go on for? No matter how hard I tried, I couldn't repair the days Dad had left broken.

Looking around the kitchen, there it was. She'd brought the gun into the house and wrapped it in the blanket and left it in the corner of the kitchen. I walked over and picked it up. Its long weight knocked against my knees.

'No,' she said. It was a command. 'Just leave it. It's his.'

'He's dead, Lesley.' Or did she mean the other guy? Her mate? 'Our father is gone.'

'But it was his. We owe him.'

'Owe him what?' This was ludicrous. Coming from her it was offensive.

'They'll find out stuff. The cops.'

'We don't know there is anything.'

'But if there is… Someone'll know.' She stomped across to me, a tea towel in her hand as if I'd interrupted her in the washing up. 'My mate'll look after it for us.'

'I don't want some guy having it.' I tugged at it.

She grabbed it and tried to twist it out of my hands. She'd worked on those wrists. The strength surprised me. Our hands were cold on the metal but hot against each other.

'Let go, or else,' she said. Jerking the rifle free at last, she shoved at my shoulder. I felt her fist in that spot where a kicking rifle bruises. She had it in her hand and was cradling it.

'Or else what?' I asked.

She just smiled, contented again. She wasn't my sister now, she was this guy's woman, a stranger in the body of a girl I grew up with. We'd never been close, but I'd always imagined I'd known her better than this. That was what scared me most, my own ignorance and complacency. But at that moment there was only this phantom woman and the rifle.

Thank God Nathan was elsewhere. But still I wanted that bigger brother badly. He'd missed the worst of the stuff, off at sport all day and sleeping at friends' houses. He was a boy. He could get away, we couldn't. I wanted to run and hide with him from this, just as I'd run to him at five years old when Dad was home. Suddenly I retched and felt the milky tea spill out of me and onto the floor.

'Shit, now we'll have to clean that up,' Lesley said. Irritated, frowning at the mess.

I slapped her freckled face, then instantly regretted it. All I could think of was the rifle with its single black eye trained on me. Grabbing my handbag, I stumbled to the back door.

'Yeah, run, you idiot.' Her voice was chasing me.

The back door swung and slammed as she followed me into the yard, then up the cracked side path to the front gate. I knew she'd have the weapon with her.

'Betray our dad, just try to, and see what happens to you.'

Glancing back, I stumbled on the crooked footpath, but not before

I saw the rifle hugged across her body and the satisfaction in her eyes. I was a kid again, I was running, running away.

Reaching my car, I scrambled in, gulped at the air which smelt of me, my real life, not the decay and stale tea of the house. Then I drove. I couldn't get the sight of her with the rifle out of my head. Rain blurred my vision but I couldn't get the windscreen wiper going. When an oncoming lorry driver rammed his horn, I saw I'd strayed across the lane, and forced myself to pull over. There was stickiness on the palm of my hand. Sniffing at it, I smelt her and rushed from the car to rub my palms into the wet weeds at the side of the road. The grass collapsed to a mat but I kept rubbing. I was at the approaches to the western motorway with its petrol station and fast food chains. Somewhere behind me another truck sprayed road water into my hair. It smelt of mud and brakes. The driver pulled over and came back to check I was all right.

There was lightning over in the south and the rain pummelled my thinning scalp as I got back into the car. I can't remember how long I drove for. The news came on and I listened without taking it in. The traffic was choked up at Olympic Park – some football game and then flash flooding from the storm. I drove on, glancing at flooded gutters, waiting to overtake broken-down cars, traffic hazard signs flashing red warnings above me. When I got home, I showered under the hottest water I could get out of it, my skin pulsing red and swollen as I got out. The storm was right above my flat, lightning flickered behind me and in the bathroom mirror. As thunder exploded overhead, I rushed to my balcony and looked up into it, daring the lightning to impale me with its charge. I'd always been afraid of storms. I'd been afraid of too much.

That was the last time I saw Lesley. I think of her sometimes with a bruised grief. In a way, it wasn't her fault. Perhaps I owed her a forgiveness. While I'd been hiding in my bedroom all those years ago, the door bolted shut, she'd been out there with Dad, taking it from him. Dad had given her the life she had, such as it was. And now he'd given her something else.

6

Fairfield

Kerry hadn't had a cigarette for two days so was it any wonder she felt like a piece of what her dad would call 'RS'. These health experts knew a lot about cancers and clinical trials but they knew nothing about the delicious relief of a cigarette.

'Skin cap?' the tiny girl behind the counter yelled.

The Vietnamese kids working in this café needed some vocal training. The confusion that reigned wasn't helped by their boredom. Probably just wanted to be back at school or studying accounting or whatever they did in their down time.

Thirteen more minutes before the meeting and audit run-through with her manager Miles, her deputy Li, and the visiting Canberra technocrats Gabby and Hong. Today, the office was full of screaming babies and smelly reluctant fathers. Why did they always choose Tuesdays to come in? Monday was shopping with the wife, Tuesday JobConnect, Wednesday coffee with the other men, Thursday lobbying with her or some other case worker who could advance their cause, wherever the queue was shortest. Friday it was the mosque, the TAB or the Leagues Club – they were all the fucking same.

'Flat why?' the waitress called.

Kerry knew by now that the missing t would be something she'd have to get used to.

Fairfield was going through the latest town upgrade, no doubt some councillor needed to spend a pile of loot before the accountants got onto him, or his business owner mate wanted to sell his shop. Oh,

Kerry, stop it, she thought! Why didn't you just stay home in bed? You've got enough sick days. Stay in bed and smoke the flat out. But she knew why she didn't – this was the day of the meeting she'd been trying to squeeze out of forever but was bound to get her. The audit rehearsal, but more importantly, the first meeting with Gabby for over a year.

A pale sun reflected off the footpath. The whiff of someone's cigarette, a road worker on his break leaning against a parking sign. She knew him, Ali or Abir, something like that, one of the genuine clients who'd really wanted a job. There he was, fluoro jacket on, and off the dole. Good on him. She caught his eye and he nodded, a weak smile. His English was zilch, but his eyes conveyed quiet satisfaction of his lot. After Kabul, the sticky gutters of Fairfield must look like heaven.

The chicken shop was taking a delivery. Water pooled where the pallets of frozen goods met the warming street. A whiff of bleach came from the just mopped shop tiles. The simple life. Ordering your stuff, cooking it, selling it, cash to the bank at four thirty every day. She sipped the coffee. Van made the best coffee, but Van didn't work Tuesdays. But Kerry didn't care today. She drank quickly, wanting the meeting to come and get its mess over with. It was a bloated pimple she wanted burst.

An announcement from the train station was echoing against the plastic hoardings, over the line, ringing its depressive official news of some delay or track work or warning of rule breaking. It carried too far, but suburban corridors did that, the unnatural disbursement of people, water, sound and smells to places they didn't belong. The awning above her was rusted and dripping condensation in a neat line six inches in from the roadway. Avoiding a woman with a herd of kids, she edged into it and felt the inevitable drip of water – right into her ear.

Fuck Fairfield! Why didn't she apply for that job in the city? She'd have had the peaceful train commute from Ashfield, all the books she could read, the respite of window shopping in the smarter strips of Castlereagh Street and the glossy palaces of Pitt Street. This job paid more, promotion was likely, but she had the hell of driving across country and parking in the stinking concrete multi-storey behind the dubious charm of the Fairfield Forum. Each morning, she hurried past the two dollar shop and the Eastern fashion emporium, the cheap crap piling to the left and right of her as the Bengali pop music drifted from the food court.

She scoffed as she walked, not caring that people heard her grunting. A weak woman, she thought, thinking of Ali from Kabul and his resigned smile. First world woman in cigarette withdrawal. She was under siege. But from what? She wouldn't dare complain to Maria or Vick or Van or to the world's loudest giggler, Rosa from Fiji. They'd laugh at her. Hell, everyone felt like that, no big deal. It was the job. She'd seen too many cases of blurred truth and muddled misconceptions, written too many recommendations for people she didn't know about issues she couldn't grasp, knowing that half of what she wrote would end up in someone's trash in head office.

She took the long way back, down the lane they called Little Baghdad. The men had packed the cafés already, the Turkish biscuit bakery was firing up the kiln at the back. The smell of hot flour escaped the wire screen door. In her early days in Fairfield she'd bought a bag of the biscuits but found them hard and tasteless and left them in the office kitchen for everyone else to eat. Those were the good old days, the days the back door was open and she could pop out with Ken and Rami for the cigarette breaks. It seemed she and the cigarette had some reverse karmic relationship. Things got worse in direct correlation to how few fags she smoked.

She dumped her empty coffee cup in the glued-up bin near the bus stop. An elegant arc of coffee splayed out from the impact, the caramel coloured droplets exploding onto the black plastic bin liner the council contractor had tucked into place. The twirl of the bin bag was a thing to behold – someone had taken pride in that knot. It reminded her of the hair knots the African kids had. She was no better than the other crappers in this suburb. Why hadn't she bought that keep cup they were selling at the café, so cute with the cats or dogs or some other endearing animal logo on them? She was too cheap, too busy, too lazy, too forgetful. Every hour was one fraught lurch to the next.

She glimpsed Gabby and Hong pushing through the front glass doors of the office twenty feet ahead of her. They'd been out planning some strategy, bonding over the bitching. The meeting would be late. Gabby had escaped Fairfield a year ago, but Kerry knew that wouldn't be the end of their 'disagreements'. Gabby had been promoted, she had some power now, some room to scratch over her past and take revenge on anyone who'd ever given her a sour word. When Gabby found out about Shane, Kerry knew there'd be no end to it. Gabby had hit the proverbial vengeful goldmine.

Kerry's desk was unusually tidy. As instructed, the case workers were holding off shunting paperwork. This was just a practice run, a dress rehearsal for the real auditor's visit where they had to look as clockwork as a German car factory. The auditors would notice in-house workloads through 'logistical stream evidence' and would recognise 'procedural noise' when they saw it. She'd made a joke about this to Li, saying Sir Humphrey would love the language of it. But Li didn't seem to get it. *Yes Minister* hadn't made it into Chinese popular culture yet.

The small conference room had been tidied up by someone – Li maybe. It occurred to her she was losing track of the simple stuff of the office these days. The Shane thing was there behind her eyes, clouding her intellect. It was never going to just slip away – office memories were long and corrosive. A snake of a client, Shane was someone she'd let herself be seen with at the pub, the git who'd tried to send her flowers. There'd been a laugh or two, a harmless coffee after work in that place which had been demolished a year ago and turned into a discount chemist. A no one, it had seemed at the time. It had turned out that Shane was an addict with a history of selling to officials in every office from Wollongong to Hornsby. Even though he'd been her client, she was the last idiot to find out. She made decisions, it was her job, she thought she was getting to know him better. He'd been the one doing the knowing. Shane was no doubt living in a caravan park in Gosford by now with five kids by three women. That was the first cig withdrawal time, the first lonely year after she'd broken up with Fabio. She'd been a big baby, a big naive fool. Shane was going to bite her in the bum big time within the hour. Gabby was going to tell Miles, she just knew it.

Gabby started it off, the usual five minutes of thanking everyone for their time and their 'incredible efforts', the obligatory nod to our 'diverse community'. Kerry remembered the first of these meetings years ago, with old Pat in charge, a community sector trooper, who'd referred to her clients as either 'Australians' or 'ethnics' with nothing much in between. In those days, Kerry remembered smoking at her desk. That seemed like a millennium ago.

There was a 'revisiting the goals of the audit strategy'. Kerry put her few cents in along the same lines, taking the lead from Gabby. She knew this dance well enough. She spoke of the value of 'informal leadership forums' such as this to 'confirm the roadmap of the organisation' and if necessary 'realign key benchmarks to ensure they were all on the same page'. On a personal note, it was always a joy to catch-up and get the 'head office goss'. Video conferences were all well and good but the team appreciated 'face to face dialogue like nothing else'. Nodding and chuckling, Gabby agreed, there was nothing more valuable than 'getting dirty back at the coalface'.

Hong, knowing it was her time to step in then, cranked up the slide show and the reports started. There the usual stream of charts and data, the lags identified with the nasty red crosses, the achievements with green ticks (Hong clearly loved PowerPoint). While she let the slides wash over her, Kerry wondered when it'd come and how – the Shane problem.

After the slides, Miles got into the swing of it. He had a tablet close and referred to it for his office reports which Kerry had produced. Bless him, he referred to his 'amazing team' and went on to outline his views on 'the way forward'. The auditors would be wanting a 'representative snapshot of the client base' which could provide a 'rounded image of service challenges and interventions.'

It was then Gabby started edging into territory which made Kerry's arms tickle. The coffee was working but this was where she needed the nicotine. The workforce support service, according to Gabby, was an area of concern – Kerry knew this was code for her. Would the auditors be scrutinising the staff-client relationships in any detail? This area 'presented unique challenges', and was 'vulnerable to volatile human factors'. Was there any risk to the organisation through the exposure to 'non-delineated governance issues' or 'inadequate boundary management'?

The shiny fake wood desk represented a fragile boundary, Kerry thought. What fool years ago in the days of money thought that would hold back an enraged community worker like her? She saw herself reach across the coffin-coloured surface and grab Gabby by her neat black jacket and slap her. Keeping her hands folded in front of her, she nodded silently and waited.

'These issues faced every corner of our sector,' Miles was saying. 'We're not unique. In a way, Gabby,' and here he leant forward, his webbed fingers knotted and hard, 'I'd be concerned if we didn't once in a while make a mistake going that extra mile for a client. We are a service about people, right?' Miles didn't sponsor the Building Effective Leadership course for nothing. He knew how to turn a sin into a virtue.

Gabby kept on. Did Miles think the audit would fold the recent Departmental Policy on Staff and Client In-confidence Guidelines into their review? This was pushing it. Miles wanted out of Fairfield as much as she did. He was looking to the next year and the regional manager's job in head office, then off to the UK, where he'd let slip he wanted to move with his English girlfriend to do the 'grand design' thing.

Miles said the department had limited resources that would be misdirected by babysitting professional staff. They'd all been trained. He had the attendance sheets to prove it if the auditors asked. Anyway, he had full confidence in 'his awesome team'.

'Well,' said Gabby, making an 'on your head' shrug.

Miles looked at her hard. He was big and could make an impression leaning across his desk with those perfectly shaved jowls glowing red.

The room got very quiet. Then he spoke in a low preachy kind of voice that kindergarten teachers use to scare the naughty kid. Stuff about everyone giving the team their 100% loyalty and possible consequences to the organisation of 'negative talk'.

Kerry hadn't seen him pissed off like this before. Whatever was going on with him, she was grateful.

They crawled through the rest of the agenda. Gabby was quiet. Miles left the room to attend, so he claimed, to some urgent emails. Hong kept the agenda churning on in her cheesy textbook way, seemingly oblivious to the sullen glances being exchanged beside her. She was too young for that job.

With Miles out of the room, Kerry flipped through a few pages, thought of nicking out for a fag. What was Miles so shitty about? Gabby and her boundaries bug had not gone down well. Maybe he knew about the Shane thing already. She laughed inside at the stupidity of it all, the games over nothing. Then a face rose from the fog behind her eyes. A face she'd made up ages ago, stored away for the fun of it, a face matching a girl called Natalia. Whatever had happened to her? A sullen Russian girl, a case to shift on. She was still on their books – Miles was going 'that extra mile' for her. Oh yes. Gabby, she thought, you've stepped on a bloody landmine.

Thinking life was too short to forgo these delicious moments, she announced she was going out for a cigarette. In a minute, she was out the back in the tiny courtyard with those delicious fumes enfolding her head. Gabby appeared. That's right, she'd been one of the nicotine crowd too.

'You quit?' Kerry asked.

'If only,' she replied.

They both laughed.

It might have been the fag, it might have been the courtyard, which had all the freedom of a prison exercise yard. Kerry opened her pack and handed one to Gabby. Clouds passed over the sun. It was a blessed relief. A hush seemed to fall over the courtyard.

'That thing,' she said. She'd try it on as she had nothing to lose. 'That thing – you know what.'

Gabby let the lighter burn unused. She had eyes the colour of a burnished hazelnut. There was a pretty youth buried under them.

'What I mean is – Miles is a nice guy basically.'

'The best.'

Kerry wasn't going to quibble. 'That thing,' she said. 'It's kinda like that fumigation they did that time at Blacktown. When they found those cockroaches in the little cupboard.'

Gabby had her mouth open. The cig was burning its lovely way down her fingers. Kerry wanted to grab it and suck the thing herself to save it. Instead, she went on and filled in the rest about the pest control people and how after the cockies they kept on and found the rats nest in someone's desk drawer. Been living there for years, apparently, on rice cracker crumbs and the water from a leaking pump under the building.

'I was there that day.' She wasn't, but it didn't matter. 'Saw them take it out. They sacked the old cleaner. He didn't go quietly, had a wife and kids. Want another one?' She passed the cigarette across. 'Men, they never do go quietly, do they?'

'Men.' Gabby drew hard and blinked.

A dollop of water fell onto the ground, then another.

'Anyway. Best leave the rats nest where it is right now. Who knows what shit's in it. There might be a big stink of the male variety.'

'Men,' she was nodding, her tongue playing at the edge of her mouth. 'Right.'

'Right.'

They squashed their butts on the paving.

As if he'd been listening, suddenly there he was, the man on both their minds, getting them back in from the smoko. Miles hated smokers. At least Kerry was trying to give it up. They stepped inside and the rain started.

Phones were ringing back in the office and some argument in Cantonese had broken out between the receptionist and a client. In the conference room, a Hungry Jack wrapper had slapped itself against the narrow strip of window at ankle height which connected the office to the street. Grease all round, in the office and out.

With Miles not saying much, Kerry pushed the meeting along, There were the clients they had to decide on parading for the auditors. How were they going to create 'the appropriate picture?' Should they close the office that day and invite the 'suitable interviewees' to a hospitality event to meet the auditors? This was something they all agreed on – their clients couldn't be exposed to auditors without 'strategic selection'. Miles spent most of the time looking at his phone, grunting his approval occasionally. There was an awful panic in Gabby's face as she tried to catch his eye.

Lunchtime crawled its miserable way to the table. Li announced she'd ordered in Turkish takeaway from the Mezza Masters opposite the station. The table in the tea room was set up for them and, no doubt warned to keep away, the office staff either stayed at their desks or went out for lunch. Kerry had never seen that plastic surface gleam. With Pat, it'd been the Liberty Rose café for schnitzel and chips. Now it was falafel, tabouli salad and baklava. Summer was coming – the tomatoes were a deep gorgeous red. Miles ate in his office. Hong and Li were comparing online shopping sites. Apparently, it was well known that the best Italian leather shoes came from Truman and Co, a Hong Kong company registered in Utah. The world was one bloody shapeless jumble sale.

The afternoon meeting was the rehearsed walk round the office with Gabby and Hong scribbling on clipboards while the clients slopped in with their tracksuits and thongs. The staff were a dream – no loose paper or football posters in sight, smart tapping at keyboards and polite replies to the usual array of incurable gripes. It's amazing how the fear of losing your job motivates people. Miles was in and out. Kerry glimpsed him in his office on the phone with the door closed. He went to uni with the manager at head office, but Gabby didn't know that. Maybe it was the phone call, maybe not, but when he emerged he went into rugby bully mode. Hands on hips and private school voice booming across the office. Kerry gave him every fact he asked for and shut up. Gabby was grey – cigarettes didn't agree with her. Their eyes meeting momentarily. Kerry gave her a flickering smile. What of Shane? Gone with the cig break long ago.

By three, they were done. Two massive folders on Kerry's desk to prove it. Miles was smirking and hurrying them out the door. What the hell was going on? A near miss, a heads-up that would save his sleazy little arse. Lucky him. Shaking hands with 'the pair', there were final ominous words about 'winning teams' and 'supporting colleagues through the next phase'. The bastard didn't care if the sad fuckers he called 'core clients' never saw a job in their entire lives. What had he done with little Natalie but shunt her from English courses to resumé writing workshops, all to make her 'job ready'? And three years later she still on the books. He'd made her into something else, had given her a horizontal career shift she'd never previously considered. Kerry couldn't wait to get to her desk and see what he'd done with her case notes. Gabby was waving, weakly smiling with desperation seeping from her lips. Too little too late. Why didn't we learn the lessons, she thought? Why did we always let them do it? The Shanes and the Mileses and the rest of them – fill our lives with the fear and anger, the desperation, the pathetic gratitude for mercy? The gratitude that it was some other woman's turn to be fucked over and not our own. Stupid women.

She waited for the cab with them huddled under the leaking awning as rain whipped around her hair. Sheet lightning came and went.

'I hope your flight's OK,' she said.

'I think I'm in for a bumpy ride.'

There eyes met and they exchanged a weak smile.

Something inside Kerry wanted to give her a kiss on the cheek, a hand grab or something. Something was owed, but not one of those girlish tokens of shared weakness. Gabby scrunched her empty cigarette box into the filthy street bin and sighed. Out.

Kerry pulled the crumpled remains of her pack from her pocket and handed it across. 'Here,' she said. 'It's my turn to give up again.'

The cab bumped over the pedestrian speed humps on Railway Parade and out to the main road, then to the airport. The view south was shrouded in the thickness of the front. Lightning emitted from its menacing blackness.

Back inside, the office was more itself. Coke cans open on desks, laughter bubbling over the blue desk petitions. They'd survived round one. She and Gabby had started in the same week over in the Blacktown office. How many cigarettes and cheap whites had they had in those pubs on the highway and how many unemployed clients had they missed lunch over and spent hours writing reports on, all to come to zilch? There were always more and always would be. Still, there were so many, they blurred, drifted further back in memory like fag butts in a flooded gutter. What was staying with her was Gabby's back getting into that cab. The private desperation hidden behind those shoulders where the black suit was pinching. There it was, the spreading evidence of fading competence, something indefinable lost. This ghost, this flicker of fading, she'd seen it at lunchtime reflected back from the mirror of the office bathroom. The flush on that once pretty cheek. Gabby's face shrank and shrank, a deflating doll shrivelling to nothing.

Thunder rumbled low out along the streets and reverberated under the rusted awnings. The courtyard was in deep shadow with a tumult pounding the steel patio table. A strange grief came over her as if she'd just glimpsed her own unwitnessed extinction.

7

Leichhardt

The second time Taylor walks past the café and sees Zan sitting in the corner table, a tremor runs through his gut. He isn't seeing things. Zan's face is the colour of a dying fish. His hair is goth, the usual, but with a bolt of white fissured down the side. He wears an insane grin.

'God it's hot,' Nancy says. She's marching slightly ahead of him with shoulders hunched. Her skin exudes the sweetness of fresh sweat.

Lean sticks of trees cramp the footpaths but are no shield from the relentless sun. Leichhardt wasn't his sort of place.

'What time did you say it starts?' Nancy asks.

'One.'

'A whole hour?'

He shrugs. She'll want to escape somewhere now and he prays something comes up ahead because he won't go back and sit in that café with Zan only a few feet away. That pained crazy grin. The cigarette packet crushed at his fingertips. The whole awful vision had been compounded by the pungent odour of burnt garlic rising from the barely concealed kitchen grill in the roof of the building.

'We can go in early,' he says. 'Look around, I guess.'

'Was that a shoe shop back there?'

Only one door back, not as far as the café. He turns like an old man and shuffles after her. The street going in the opposite direction is just as hot. In the distance, the main road swims with heat, the cars are flashes of black, white, pausing with the lights, a front of colour advances as people cross the road. He'd dreamt of Zan that morning, the two of them together in Leichhardt ten years ago, and he guessed it meant something. Especially with Zan squatting in a café not twenty yards away.

The shoe shop has the glue from removed fittings on the walls, flapping handwritten signs, synthetic tablecloths dragging on the thin carpet.

'These are too cheap.' Nancy's voice sly, her mouth a leer along the stacked parade of shoes.

The trestle tables have been lined up one next to another, the shoes on grim show like bodies exhumed from a mass grave. At the back of the store a fat man perches on a stool, his white shirt pinched at his belt. Knowing Nancy isn't planning to buy anything, he avoids the man's eye.

Outside, a hot wind has gone through the stooped bottlebrush. Pink stamens litter the grills of cars and the fine cracks in the footpath.

'You wanna go in?'

This time she shrugs and leads him into the bookshop next door. Fluttering tides of cold air tickle his ears as the door opens. The smell of clean paper, coffee, new furniture. Somewhere round here he and Zan had once spent an hour in a bookshop. An hour killing time before something other than a movie. The sort of place which had never seen a broom. Deep in the shelves, a girl with a cold had snuffled through some paperbacks. Zan in the T-shirt which was black like his hair. Grabbing at Zan's hand, he'd felt his shiver and a slick of cold sweat infused with hand cream. Zan's eczema had bloomed under the stress. They'd both been scared, but neither of them about to admit it. They'd checked out the house, which was down a mean side street where kids on bikes circling outside, a cat asleep on a brick fence. Shifting his weight, the cheap floorboards had creaked and in his head the kids circled, round and round, right at the door of the house. The kids had made him nervous. Maybe that'd been the problem.

A high-pitched digital bell sounds as someone tries to leave via the fire exit.

'Excuse me,' the girl at the counter almost as loud as the door. Frowning, her palms gripping the corner of her counter sanctuary.

Everyone looks, the offender mutters something, sorry maybe, his bald head bobs to the real door and is away down the road.

'They should have a bigger sign,' Nancy says.

For the first time, he notices her hair, the way she's had it cut and dyed that pulsing bronze. She's done it for him and he's barely looked at her all morning.

'You want a drink before we go in? Hot out.'

Hands in his pockets, he stands closer to her. Plenty of room, the place a hanger of reflected daylight, aisle after aisle of clean paper, covers as sleek as a car dealership. As she turns to face him, the street glare hits her and the pores of her skin and the tiny colony of pimples at her hairline are exposed in brilliant detail. Not beautiful in the normal way, her features are compact, the nose and chin stubby, her smile producing plump roses in her cheeks. There is expectancy and a confronting openness in her eyes. He feels unjustly privileged.

'I wish I could stay in here all day,' she says. 'Don't you?'

He does but maybe for a different reason. When she moves to the door, he pulls the book she's spent ages pouring over off the shelf and takes it to the counter. Small and compact in its clean paper bag, the spine seems to be made to fit the palm of his hand.

Outside, a group of women, Italian oldies, amble around them on their way into a restaurant. Hot wind whips the odour of their makeup and hairspray to his nose. One of them has a cake in a box. A little girl in a holy communion dress rushes from within the restaurant to take it from her, standing on tiptoes to keep it from falling. Cheers from inside, the men with beers in front of them are pleased to see the women or the cake, he can't tell which. It's a Sunday in Leichhardt and he can't be part of it. He's on the other side of a life window to these people – the families, the swaggering kids, the old widowers with dogs who sit reading the Italian newspapers on their verandas.

'Oh, you got something,' says Nancy. 'What?'

'For you.'

'Huh?' It's getting late and as she walks she tears open the bag. She stops at the bus stop to look at it properly. 'But I've read this. Why did you buy this?'

'Thought you might like it… It was just a thought.'

The whirring hum of the bus, a crowd surging at the door and more cool air washing him. For a second, they're in the crowd, shouting into the ears of a stranger only inches away. A girl with too many piercings pretends she's not hearing Nancy's nasally query.

'But you know I hate Bukowski.'

'Yeah, still…' Had she told him this fact? Maybe some point-scoring on her part.

It'd be as hot as a barbecue where Zan was sitting. He'd had a whole pack of cigarettes in front of him, he was sure their eyes had met. He wondered what Zan would make of him. Such a clean guy now, an ironed shirt, a non-smoker. Maybe to Zan's eyes invisible. A mercy then. Summer had never been his season. Here was another case in point. The sight of Zan slammed hard into his head and stuck fast.

The queue is a long one – holidays still, teenagers with popcorn boxes too large to hold, women sitting along the walls in pairs, an industrial strength fan no match for an air conditioner. Somewhere off in the distance a plane making a descent.

He'd resealed the tape to the bag. The shop'll stay open, Nancy said, might as well take it back straight away. Not meeting his eye now, she's still sore over the Bukowski.

The film passes like the nothing of a dreamless sleep. He's blissfully alone, the air in the cinema temple cool and inducing clarity in him. The bodies around him are mere statues – aloof, non-judgemental, he wants only their company from now on, but the real world is not going away any time soon.

As the credits roll up, so too does Zan's face and the hunched corner, the dazed grin and glassy eyes. He was crazy to have come back to Leichhardt. He dreamt badly and should have known what that meant.

Back on the street, the wind is high, a bushfire is burning somewhere up north. It'd been on the news coming in the car. They'd talked about it as he'd parked the car, then they'd moved onto the environment, politics, laughed at that then moved onto something else. So easy, the whole morning fluid, the rising heat invigorating on the back of his arm as it rested on the window ledge.

'We're going to get rain, thank God.' Nancy flaps at the air then notices droplets searing the parched footpath.

He blinks at the spot and sees nothing but their shadows and the swift wheel of a passing pushbike. Back past the café, empty now, the whole front section is now shaded by an awning with a beer commercial on its face. No Zan.

'Are you coming?' Nancy takes off the sunglasses now that the sky has darkened and she's frowning at him. Her hair is a helmet too heavy for her delicate skull. All for him and he isn't worth it.

'Sorry, just looking for something.'

'What?'

A bus coming in the opposite direction pulls up and the movie crowd start to pile in. It takes time, there's a crush at the door, no one willing to give way. A guy with his girlfriend sweats under the weight of a leather jacket before giving in and shedding it. Must be trying to impress. He'd done that kinda thing once but hadn't tried with Nancy. He supposed that said something.

Searching the heads, he catches his breath – a splash of white, a gaunt black shirted man climbing the stairs of the bus. Then the press of the crowd, a bad ad for the movie they've just seen plastering the side of the bus which roars off then shrieks to a stop at the orange light. A hoon car turns a corner and slows in the traffic, its monstrous engine throbbing and spluttering fumes.

'What now?' Nancy's voice is brittle with irritation. 'I hope it hits soon, don't you?'

He's gone to the kerb and is leaning into the roadway, but it's too hard to see – he's just an accident statistic waiting to happen. He should answer her, give her that courtesy. But then there should be more. About what had happened to him and, he supposed, Zan too. They were not five minutes from the street where he'd left him all those years ago. In the house with the tarp roof and the broken back door where the deal had happened. Zan, too desperate to wait, drifting out of consciousness on the greasy couch. A day like this with a hot stinking wind roaring down the gloomy corridor. It'd been someone's home once, one of those families with kids playing in the sizzling roadway. Fallen wallpaper, obscene graffiti on the ornate cornices – how the hell had that happened? He'd thought at the time, handing over money to the guy with the black depthless eyes, why did they have to do that? Then the sirens, the terror of that bad trip, the night lying in the gutter with the ants crawling in his armpits and the cats pissing against the stone wall of the lane way.

'Can we get a drink?'

The driver of the throbbing car thinks he's been spoken to and stares.

'Yeah, OK,' says Nancy. 'Why?'

'I'm thirsty. Isn't that enough?'

Clearly it isn't and he can't blame her. Almost in unison, they pull at their sticky shirts. The first communion party is breaking up. Kids are starting to scream as they do when it gets windy and a change in weather comes. A long sedan drives past towards Parramatta Road with the little girl in the white dress up front. She sucks on an iceblock which is melting too fast and dribbling onto her frock. As they pass the street, he doesn't look down there, but can't help feeling the tug of the cooled air as it runs up from the valley at the bottom of the street. There is thunder somewhere. He can't help associating it with some impending justice. He deserves to feel the pain of it, a lightning strike perhaps, but that's too sudden, too merciful. The trees are mature, so they must have been there ten years ago, but he has no memory of them. He should at least walk past the house and stop. A hollow gesture of remembrance, but better than nothing.

'So what's eating you?' Nancy asks.

'It's complicated.'

'So?' Exasperated. Like him, worn out in the heat.

He could love her maybe, if he tried, and he needs to tell someone. Maybe she'd understand, or even just forgive him. But that wasn't possible. Only Zan could do that.

'I hate Leichhardt,' he says. 'I just… Hate it.'

'Me too. So?'

He wants to say it then – 'Because I left a guy to die down there, about twenty yards away. Too scared to call the ambulance. I even hid when the cops came.' And then, the mad bit, 'And I just saw him back in that café.'

Instead, he shakes his head. 'I think I'm losing it, Nancy.'

'You'd better tell me then.'

He figures she'd make a good counsellor.

'Putting things away, not looking, it doesn't work, does it?'

There is a coolness down his back. It is raining, nice and hard and cleansing. This is it. If he can't tell it now, when can he?

'That Bukowski,' she says, looking up into his face. Rain is sitting on her mascara like miniature soap bubbles. It is beautiful and miraculous. 'I was making it up. I've never read it. I was angry. See? It's not hard to confess.'

'You make it easy, Nancy. Not everyone can do that.'

'I don't love you, by the way.'

'You've made your point.'

'Rain brings stuff out – do you still want that drink?'

'After the rain. I need the rain.' He is soaked through. But it's not enough.

'OK, then the drink – then after that you'll tell me.'

'Yeah, sure,' he lies. 'Yeah, Nancy, then I'll tell you all about it.'

8

Mosman

She'd heard Larry call it debris, but to Margery it was just plain litter. The Trentons were no doubt billionaires, but they couldn't keep five metres of roadway clean. An empty cement bag twisted and damp under foot, broken palm fronds, the ubiquitous cigarette butts. They'd blame the builders no doubt. A quick glance back at her own house – trees a bit overgrown, but the lawn impeccable, the edges of her paths weed free. Inside, the windows shut, the curtains drawn, Hetty the cat probably still asleep at the back garden window. If she ever renovated her house, she'd never take this long.

'So the end of the noisy work is in sight then,' she asked Evelyn Trenton.

They were standing in front of the Trentons' massive house on the good side of the road which ran down to the harbour. It was a decent street. When Margery gave her address to tradesmen and shopkeepers, that's how she described it. A decent street.

A cement mixer was reversing back and forth a few houses up. Trying to squeeze in to do the Trentons' driveway, which had been pummelled to a wreck of stones.

'Your dogs can't be enjoying this. The dust, the noise, bad for them. Aren't you worried about them?'

'Oh, nonsense.' Evelyn scoffed through her skinny neck. Seventy years old and she saw nothing wrong with wearing pink gym clothes. 'They love the action. Working dogs, Margery. That's what they've always been. Working dogs. The best kind. They don't run off and leave, unlike cats. Those animals….'

'What, those are working dogs?' Margery prompted, her head tipped inquisitively to the side. 'The city's not much of a place for working dogs, Evelyn. I've seen Larry out walking them at all hours. They must be bored silly.' Tentative laughter, not echoed by Evelyn.

Peering down through the shrubs, she saw the tips of Evelyn's topiary garden. There was gurgling from a water feature somewhere in there. But Margery had never seen it. She'd never set foot inside that garden.

'They used to be working dogs,' said Evelyn. 'On the farm. We did sheep, you see. On twelve thousand acres down south. The dogs loved it.' Her hard lips peered at the fence that kept the dogs in. Whining, wanting out. 'They're good mutts. Getting on in years, that's all.'

She stepped to the gate, flicked the top catch and out they came, stalking through the dust, chewing on the hessian sand bags left to soak up the water from the stone cutters.

Margery felt her feet go leaden. She wasn't a dog person, hadn't liked them since she'd been twelve years old and bitten by a Maltese terrier. Evelyn had let them out on purpose.

'That's Blackie, the Lab, and the kelpie cross is Gregory,' said Evelyn. 'He's named after my eldest boy. In Dubai now.' Hard laughter. 'Money market. Miss him.'

'Beautiful coat on him,' Margery admitted, holding her breath. Reduced to cowardice.

Gregory circled and sniffed. Passing her feet, he licked at a piece of loose grass caught in her laces. A tremor ran across her chest.

'Hey you,' ordered Evelyn. 'Gregory. Back here. Quick.'

At least Evelyn had trained them well. Her phone rang and she took it. Her builder, fifteen minutes late and stuck in traffic. Mid-December and it could have been February. The sun searing along the footpaths, into Margery's uncovered thinning scalp. She'd had a good head of hair once. In the years when Reg had been alive. Swallowing, she pressed on, refusing to look at the dogs.

'A full year now since you started, Evelyn. Been a bit of a… Mess really. The trees, the water main ruptured that day…'

'Oh that.' Her head flung back. A bit of a joke.

'That crane you brought in was parked in the street for so long grass was growing around its base. Must have cost a fortune not being used for all that time. I suppose the timing is hard to get right, but still…'

'That was the architect's fault. Got the timeline wrong. Should have gone with my man, but Larry liked him. Trust a man to use some mate at the golf course as a recommendation. Men.' A grunt and her hand perched on her hip. A tanned leg peeked from the bottom of her gym pants. She spent too long in the sun.

'The expense – it must worry you. This whole business.' Keeping annoyance from her voice, Margery scoured the house and the road, thought of the potholes, the scratched cars, the damaged tree branches, the polluting runoff in the gutters. All this woman's doing. 'I wouldn't have coped with it, but you… Apart from the inconvenience. A whole year of it, so far…'

'Oh, has it been that long? I hadn't noticed. But the council.' Evelyn shook her head, fanned hard little nails through the air. 'Bastards every one of them. We've done everything they asked for. Reduced the roofline, shortened the windows, got a bloody heritage consultant in. Cost a fortune. And they're still carrying on. It's a disgrace – we live in a nanny state, Margery, a bloody nanny state.'

'So I suppose you can afford the delay then.' She pulled at her shopping basket, manoeuvred around the dogs, over the kerb which was crumbling away beneath her.

She wanted to move off, get the shopping done. There were clouds building up, she didn't want to get caught. If she had that kind of money, she'd buy a little cottage by the water and potter. That should be enough for anyone. What did they want with that mansion, at their age, just the two of them, rattling around, lording it over the street? There was the housework for one thing, but then Evelyn would have cleaners…

'The money isn't the issue, Margery. Larry worked hard on that farm. Me too for that matter. We'd always promised ourselves a place by the water one day.'

'But a year to build a couple of rooms.' The trolley on the higher, undamaged ground now, she felt better. 'I've had cracking along my side path. The drilling, you see. It's possible…'

'Oh, nonsense. Your place is just old, Margery. Old.' The word dragged out to a moan.

'But well built. Not like today. Not like…'

She cast a glance at the half-finished roof, the French window looking into the yard where that young couple lived, the ones who were never home when she knocked. She'd tried five times now. She'd slipped a note under their door, but that'd been a month ago and nothing, not a word, not a quick scrawled reply on an inch of paper. She'd taken her hand-drawn petition, copied word for word from the *Citizen's Action Handbook* she'd borrowed from the library, up and down Vista Drive. She had two signatures – one from the old Greek woman who complained about everything and one from her best friend Millicent who was in the early stages of dementia.

'I suppose you realise that laneway will flood when it rains. No grass to soak it up. Grass is very important, Evelyn. And trees.'

'Oh, rubbish, it won't flood. It's all planned, Margery, underground tanks, drains, all high tech. You're just cross about the tree, that's all.'

The dogs patrolled the gutters, cocked their legs against the timber fence Reg had built with his own hands. Evelyn had hit a raw nerve there. If she tried, Margery could still smell the delicious mulch from those leaves as they bedded down in her compost bin. It had taken her an hour every Saturday to collect them, but her roses were now the best in the street.

'There was nothing wrong with that tree.' Her voice quivering despite herself. She had the walk to the shops to manage and only a single hanky in her pocket. As always, tears were a nuisance. 'And anyway, there's a tree protection order in the by-laws. I've read it.'

'Oh, you would.' Evelyn leaned around her and called up the road to the cement man. 'You've got room, Sam. Larry's gone to the office, his spot's free.' Her voice spewed up the narrow road, as insidious as the dust. 'Look, the tree was a pest and the council agreed. At least on that point, they saw sense. So all those letters you wrote were a waste of time. Oh yes, I saw them.' A nasty curl cut across her lips.

Margery picked at the rust which bled along the handle of her trolley.

'The file is on the public record, you know, Margery.'

As she raised her voice, the dogs started to bark. A wet panting as Gregory brushed her leg. Hetty had started to brush against her legs at nights as they got ready for bed. But a cat was different.

'Oh well,' she shrugged. Starting to move off, the trolley ground against a dropped screw. The street was littered with them. 'I've got nothing to be ashamed of. It's been a disruptive business all round. Everyone thinks so.'

'Who? Who thinks so except you? Show me the names.'

'Not everyone's as brave as me. As assertive as I am, what with the letters and everything.'

'You can't get anyone to agree with you. No one does. This is all temporary and building work is messy. So what? Come on, Sam!' shouting up the hill again, but the man at the cement mixer was lazy, fiddling around at his tyres as if looking for a puncture. Probably scared off by the shouting. Another coward in the street. 'So why, if you're so brave and assertive, didn't you just come over and knock on our door, Margery? Why the letters? In the country, no one behaves like that. People talk. Sort it out over a cuppa. Hmm?'

Blackie was sniffing at her leg, and Evelyn had pulled him over to scratch at his head. She was bow-legged, the back of her hands still purple with cold even in this sun. Old and looking it.

'I'm entitled to have my say,' said Margery. 'And I didn't expect much of a reception from you or Larry. Not after the tree business.'

'And you were wrong about the tree – it wasn't a haven for wildlife. It was a pest. We'll plant something else.'

'My cat used to climb it.'

'A cat isn't wildlife. Anyway, I didn't know you had a cat.' Picking up the dog's droppings in a plastic bag, she missed the blanching across Margery's face.

Margery had to get to the shops before it was too late. 'Er, she's dead now. Nancy. She was a tabby.'

'Oh dear. How long ago?' She stood and looked at Margery straight on.

As Evelyn pulled the pink gym coat close around her, Margery caught a glimpse of her sunken chest. 'A few years ago now.'

She thought of old Nancy run over by the boy in the van, the son of the family up the road. What could she do? A year of bitterness. And now Hetty, in front of the newly installed gas fire – she'd love it when winter came. The trees kept that sitting room cold and, with Reg gone, she could have it on all year round without having to explain herself to anyone. Hetty's little head rising to be patted. All those lonely nights, the sound of the Trentons and their busy shouting, the dogs bounding against the fence, the clattering of the grandkids bikes and toys on the paving. One less animal in their yard would make so little difference to them. Margery deserved Hetty. She'd never have a mansion, a dog, a grandchild.

'I had a cat. Not long ago.' As Evelyn spoke, she opened the gate again and whistled. A country noise, a curling whip of a thing like the tail of a lyrebird. 'Come on, Blackie, Gregory. Rain coming.'

The dogs obeyed. A flash of sheen from the black dog's coat as it disappeared. The soft scratch of their claws from over the fence.

'She went missing. A few months ago. Like I said, cats, they're...'

'Oh?' Margery felt a chill run through her. She told herself it was the cool change approaching.

'Run over maybe? Or taken? I don't know.' Evelyn's lowered blinking eyes, then a gruff explosion of noise which might have been a word. 'Never mind. That's cats for you.'

The cement truck reversed, its wheels grinding loose roadway. The handle of Margery's shopping trolley was scalding hot.

'How's your younger son?' It came from her unexpectedly. She didn't feel like shopping now. There was lightning about and she had a morbid fear of being struck. 'The one with the broken leg... He's still in that cast. It's been weeks.'

'Oh, that. He was fixing a fence down on the farm for us. He'll recover. Young, you know.'

Awkwardness. The ferocious ripping of Evelyn dealing with her junk mail. The rain started. The envelopes in Evelyn's hands turned dark grey with water. It didn't seem to bother her. Margery wasn't going to apologise. What for? A few letters sent? A bit late for that now. And to admit there was something more to make amends for, that she had anything else to regret, which she didn't. Heaven forgive her, she didn't.

'If you don't mind, he's got to get in here,' said Evelyn.

The truck, of course. It finally edged its way to the driveway. The driver a mere boy with a thousand jobs ahead of him.

Walking up the hill, she felt the rain getting heavier. Pulling out her umbrella, she pushed it open just as a great gust of wind tore at its fibres, twisting its metal skeleton to pieces. It hung useless in her hands and water started to pour into the open trolley. Thank God Hetty was inside. The cat had settled into her quiet shady house, an indoor cat now, safe from cars and possums and intestinal worms. Spoilt rotten, if the truth be told, consuming cans of sardines and turkey neck, lactose-free snacks, slivers of Margery's own meat portions spooned to the floor under the dining table.

She looked down to the big house – Evelyn was gone. She had no doubt Evelyn would be peering out from behind those curtains, watching the bedraggled state of her fumbling on the rainswept hillside. Fork lightning shot from the cloud across the harbour. Water trickled down her neck and ran from her limp fringe. There was no justice in the world. There would always be those 'with' and those 'without' and those stuck in the rain and those not. Finding her hankie, she blew her nose. It was useless, the cloth a sodden mess already. After shopping, she'd go to the hairdresser and also to that nice homewares store with the big coloured umbrellas. She might even stop at that place that made the little custard tarts and sit inside out of the rain. She smiled to herself – after all that, she'd toddle home where she still had Hetty. And there was nothing Evelyn could do about it. Thunder roared towards her turned back, she took a deep breath and stomped uphill.

9

Liverpool

Omar went to the window every five seconds, he couldn't help it.

'Get away, Omar, you're an idiot.' His sister was trying to feed Aisha. The baby hadn't slept since yesterday, everyone was going mad with the noise. And now this. 'They might see you looking. They'll come.'

'They'll come here anyway, doesn't matter. Anyway, I wanna see what's happening.'

'Is it a robbery?'

He was hungry and his mother was going to get food, then getting distracted and coming out again without doing anything. He was going to drive her to Liverpool markets so she could buy nuts. Aunty Rema would be waiting. There were no cars out on the street. He was sure they'd be tracking the phone, so he didn't text. The boys would be wondering where he was by now. Soccer practice had started at nine. Here they were just after ten and still stuck inside.

A dog was barking. Lucy, the Newton's staffy, three doors down — she got stressed at the sound of a doorbell. She'd be in the backyard under the carport. Mr Newtown did the night shift on the trains. His wife was in Bali on some yoga retreat.

'Can you see anything?' Mali was jigging Aisha and the baby was crying now.

'Thought you said I couldn't see anything from here?' He was the one at the window, not her.

'Yeah, well, maybe.'

The lawns were curling in the heat and cars were parked on most front yards and the sun was reflecting off the bonnets. Across the road was the huge brick mansion those Yugoslavs had built a year ago with the double garage and the pool out back. Someone was swimming in it, he could hear the echo of kids voices off water and tiles. The palm trees they'd planted at the side were sagging, the tips yellowing. The mother, he didn't know her name, she hosed the garden most nights, even last night when rain had been forecast. Motorbikes visited the house next to theirs. He bet it was Nomads but could they have been Comancheros? He kept away from those mean fuckers. He wasn't saying anything to the cops about them. They had to live opposite.

'Where is he?' he said, meaning his father. Leaving the window, he flopped onto the sofa next to Mali. His mother jerked her head up – her husband was in the bedroom praying. When wasn't he? Omar used to go up with him to pray, but not any more.

'Allah will provide,' he'd say when he came down. The old man never said anything else.

Omar took Aisha and rocked her on his knees. It worked sometimes. He loved the sight of her little eyes drying out after a good cry.

There were steps and voices outside and next door's electric doorbell rang. It played some English song from old days. They all jumped at the sound. The cops were inside now talking to the Tamils who lived there. The Tamils were always frowning and trimming their shrubs and washing that big sedan. The son was doing law at the uni. Whenever he saw Omar he had a curl at the side of his mouth. They'd talk nice to the cops and have plenty to say about everyone.

Omar gave Aisha back to Mali and hurried to the back door and held the bead screen to stop the noise, then listened hard. Nothing. Cicadas were starting up in the sagging gums that lined the canal. His dad kept saying he'd have those trees cut down if he had his way. There were bats in there during summer, and they did nothing but make a mess on the footpaths and drop bits of half-eaten fruit over everything. Omar didn't talk back to the old man, but he liked the bats. There'd been a Parks and Wildlife guy come to the school once and he'd brought a small brown animal snuggled into a baby's blanket. They'd crowded round, looked but not touched. It had squeaked and twitched and had pink ears.

Thank Allah it was Sunday and there was no TAFE. Omar missing class would be something else his dad would complain about.

They'd heard the shots at around two in the morning. Omar had never heard that sound before. If he'd gone with Malik to Turkey, by now he'd have heard it. By now, he might have fired a machine gun, he might have – he tried to stop thinking about it. Malik had been his best friend. He'd seen his Facebook brags, had even Liked some.

His dad upstairs, he prayed hard, but he had no idea. He was an old man. His father had said to forget Malik. His father had said to pray. But when Omar prayed, a black hole appeared in his soul, like those coal mines everyone hates.

'Omar?' Mali was standing in the hall holding Aisha. 'Omar? Go ask them to hurry up.'

'As if.'

'What will they want with us?,' his sister asked.

'They're going to all the houses. About the… Whatever it was.'

'How long will it take?'

He shrugged.

'I want to go out.'

'What am I supposed to do?' She should be trying to feed Aisha. 'Take Aisha and lie down.'

'Well, get the fan for me, will you?'

'In a minute.' The back screen door whined, so he let it shut – he didn't want them to think he was listening in.

'Omar,' she was scared. 'Aisha needs nappies, I need to go to the shops. Go and see if we can get out.'

'Not now, Mali.'

She sighed. She was always sighing. She expected him to do everything, the stuff Malik should be doing. If only she hadn't married him – Malik. He'd failed his sister, and now she had that fucker's child. They were brothers for life, it was Allah's curse on them all.

He got the fan out and set it up in the bedroom Mali shared with her mother and the baby. It was going to be a hot one. When the cops had been, he'd ring up the brothers and head off to the movies or maybe the gym.

A skink had snuck into the kitchen. He swept it outside with a tea towel, where a magpie swooped and got it in a second flat. That was life, just chance – one lives and one dies. He could have gone with Malik, he'd seen the videos, he'd prayed. He'd been online about to buy tickets, but at the last minute, he'd stopped. His mind kept drifting back. He had to look forward, forget Malik. But then he saw Aisha, the baby and his pudgy nose. Because of him, because Malik had been his friend, he'd approved of the marriage. His parents agreed too. The bastard had deceived them all, and now Mali was without a husband.

The cops were out front now. He ran to look between the curtains again. They were writing in notebooks. One guy was bald and was chewing gum, the other was a red head with a sharp number one haircut and a tattoo on his forearm with a dragon on it. He was standing with his back to the window talking on a walkie-talkie. He walked into the road and started waving back up towards the roundabout. An ambulance drove past – quiet, no sirens. Nothing. Two women came out of the house opposite – the Nomad house. One was crying. His mother put a hankie to her mouth.

Then the cops were at their door.

'We don't know them,' his mother rasped. 'We don't know.' She was shaking her head, looking at the carpet.

'Go make some coffee, Mum,' he said.

They were giants in the cramped room. Both of them were over six feet. They smelt of chewing gum and aftershave. Omar asked them to sit down and they chose the straight dining chairs, not the couch. He sat on the couch and they seemed to loom over him.

The older bald one introduced himself as Sergeant Gabriani. He had a tight smile which came and went. 'We'd like to talk to everyone here, if that's OK.'

'My dad's praying upstairs,' Omar said.

'We'd like to speak to him anyway, thanks.'

His mother went to get him. Their voices floated down the stairs talking in muffled Arabic. The old man didn't want to know, he was saying it was nothing to do with them. As if the cops would take that. Omar wasn't ready to head this household, but it was coming, had been coming since Malik left. Malik was his age and Malik had gone to war.

When his dad came down, he kept calling them sirs in his bad English and reported on how hard he'd been praying. As if they cared. The whole family fell in place along the long sofa and looked up at the cops.

The sergeant gave them the story straight away. He was sober, he was a professional. The guy's laser-blue eyes drilled down into Omar and he felt a chill despite the growing heat. It was Mr Chan from number 8. Shot at close range at two a.m. His son was injured. There were others too. The sergeant said their identities were 'yet to be known'.

In his mind, Omar saw Mr Chan's stooped figure driving past in his car, the white Toyota Camry, saw him collecting his mail while yelling on his mobile in Chinese, passing the takeaway containers to his daughter Louise on the Friday nights after the long drive from Penrith, where he ran an electrical store.

His mother started rocking back and forth on the lounge. She'd start crying any second. She liked Mrs Chan and knew Louise.

They wanted to know all sorts of stuff. How long had they known the Chans? How often did they see them? Had they ever been in the Chan house? Had they ever met anyone in the house? Had they ever seen anyone other than the family? Omar tried to answer for them, especially his mum. She had started praying under her breath in Arabic. His father was speaking fast about the street and how the police never came unless there was trouble, no one knew anyone any more, in his village he knew everyone, there was never trouble. That was shit – there was war in his village, what else was that but trouble? Omar tried to shut him up. The cops didn't want that, they kept asking him to translate. He tried to say the old man was rambling, saying nothing, but that wasn't right. The cops weren't stupid.

Aisha started crying again. Between his father and the baby and the cops with the steely eyes, he felt his heart pumping against his chest. With each question and answer, he started to raise his voice. It was dumb and he knew it, but he couldn't help it. He couldn't leave the couch, it would look rude. Instead, he slumped down and flung his arms above his head and let off the F word. Dumb.

'Omar.' This time it was the younger cop. 'This has been a harrowing morning. But we need you to answer a few more questions for us.'

'I don't know anything!' He didn't mean to yell.

His father shook a fist at him and told him to pull his head in. He told his father to shut up.

'Omar, we understand you've only been in the Liverpool area a year,' the pale cop said. 'Is that correct?'

'Yeah, that's right.'

'And where were you before?'

'Casula.'

'Public housing?'

'What's it matter?'

'Are you at school or working?'

'TAFE. Mechanics.'

'And school? Casula?'

He nodded.

Then they asked about Casula, school stuff, the mosque. He should bring the fan in. He was sticking to the couch with sweat. His left leg was jigging. He tugged at his soccer sleeve and pulled it up to his elbow. He saw his skinny wrists and the one still stained thumb from the workshop on Friday. A four-wheel drive with a crap engine he'd been cleaning. When he got a good job, he'd get a decent car, not the crap he worked on.

'What's this got to do with the Chans?' he asked.

Just standard procedure, they said.

'What they want, Omar?' his father was asking. Poor bastard couldn't follow, he was fumbling with his beads and his face was an orange colour. Humiliated in his own house. If only the cops would talk to him direct. He was the father here.

'So, getting back to Mr Chan,' said Gabriani, flicking the pages of his notebook. 'You said you'd didn't really know him. And the rest of the family?'

'He was a neighbour, that's all.'

'But you said,' pages flicking back and forth, 'your mother knew Mrs Chan?'

'Oh, yeah.'

'And you, miss?' He leant over and directed his question to Mali. 'What do you know of the family?'

'She doesn't know, don't speak to her!' It was his father again, upset they were interrogating his daughter.

The cops ignored him.

'What's your name, miss?'

'She no miss!' his father blurted out in English.

The cops looked at the old man.

'So, Mr Khalid, you do speak some English?'

'Small,' he said. 'No Chan, no family!' He waved his arm and his attempt at English told Omar how annoyed he was. He wasn't proud of his English and only used it when he had to.

'Miss, what's your name?'

'My baby needs new nappies.' She sighed loudly and shifted the baby from one knee to another. 'I gotta go to the shops.'

'Yes, miss, sure, this won't take very long.'

'Yeah, I know, but like, how long? Mum and I go together most days, and now, see my baby, she's crying.'

Aisha started wailing. Mali held the wriggly body up between herself and the cop.

'Where is the father of your baby, miss?'

Mali looked at her brother. 'Omar, tell them I've gotta go. I'm not talking about him.'

'They want that fucker!' his father yelled into Omar's face.

'No!' Omar answered.

'Omar, can you translate please?' It was the young one.

'My sister's husband, he's overseas.'

'And what's his name, Omar?'

He locked eyes with the man and felt his soul peel open in front of them. Malik. He heard himself mouth the fucker's name under his breath. The other cop was typing it into his mobile.

Omar breathed deep and looked at the palms of his hands. He shouldn't. They say that makes you look guilty. He looked up and they were still watching him. His mother started yelling at his father – what sort of men keep a baby in wet nappies like this? She pushed herself from the couch and grabbed her handbag, went into the kitchen and called Aunty Rema on her mobile.

'Maam, if you could wait…' Gabriani stopped and turned to Omar. 'Omar, who is she calling?'

'Mum!' he called. She wasn't listening. 'Mum!' He marched in and grabbed the phone. 'They don't like it, Mum. Later!'

'They have no right to be here, questioning us! Mali needs nappies.'

'Mum, Mr Chan is dead!'

Her stubby hands came across her face and she was about to cry again. 'This is just the beginning, Omar. Mr Chan, I am sad for them…' She shook her head and pounded her chest. 'But you are my son!'

It had nothing to do with him. It was the Chans. But it wasn't just that and he knew it.

'Mum, I'm fine. Just keep off the phone, will you?'

'You should go. As soon as they leave this house, you go.' It was as if she'd read his mind.

'That just looks worse, Mum. They're looking for some guy, whoever did it.'

'Ah, it's those bikies, or some triad thing, we don't know.'

'Mum…'

He sighed and glanced back at the cops. The young cop with the red hair was reading something on a Blackberry.

A translator had arrived. When she opened her mouth, his father muttered under his breath – Lebanese. The young cop took the translator and his mother to the kitchen while Gabriani kept going on at Omar and his dad. They went around in circles. They were back onto school again, Casula, the gym, then back to the street. He told them about the bikies. They nodded and took notes. He said they knew the Chans to nod at but that was all.

'Do you know of any possibly illegal activities occurring in your street, Omar?'

Did they mean the Chans? Drugs? He'd never touched that shit, he was proud of that. Did they mean the Nomads? Maybe. He felt energy drain from his shoulders. How long would this go on for? Without asking, the silent one went to the backyard and walked around the fence, peering over the palings. Omar heard his walkie-talkie squeaking every few minutes. What were they looking for?

When they finally left, it took him by surprise. His father stood up and saw them out, all the time calling them sirs and saying how they had nothing to do with those Chinese. Omar told the cops his dad was upset and rambling. He was ashamed of himself for the lie.

It'd been forty minutes. Longer than with the Tamils. The bikie family were watching him. The air was still, down south clouds were thickening with a yellowy tinge at the edges. He hoped the weather held for soccer.

He took his mum and Mali to the shops. The car throbbed in the traffic. He double-parked in the bus zone and bought a coffee then went to the gym and parked in the crowded underground parking bays. The boys were there and he told them about the Chans. While he lifted weights, he couldn't forget it. If Malik had been there, he'd have talked to him about it. Towelling off he went onto Facebook and made a post on Malik's wall. Something glib, a shrug into the cloud. What the fuck did he care about Malik? The bastard, the brother, the gone husband and father, an egotistical dickhead. You've put a hole in me, he said to himself, peering down at the dumb photo of Malik in some camp in Libya. You've put a hole in me.

Outside, it was getting darker by the minute. He walked and waited for soccer practice time. The gate at the mosque was open. Inside, people were kneeling like his father. A car beeped to make him move. A shiny green Mazda – Malaysians inside, their neat beards and starched shirts spotless in the air-conditioned vehicle. A girl in the back seat was on her phone, her nails sharp and gleaming in red. He didn't know them. He knew none of them. He'd left his mates in Casula and saw less of them every week. He walked on. Next week, he'd go to the Chans and leave flowers from the family. His mum would visit Mrs Chan when the time was right. Water spattered the footpath in front of him and a couple of green birds flicked past him making a noise. They got loud when a storm was coming. They knew stuff people didn't.

The cop car rounded the corner and slowed down. White and clean, it glowed against the blackening sky. He took off his sunglasses to see through the gloom. The men's eyes were still shielded. Their hair was short, one was chewing gum, one was wearing a suit. Fuck, how hot must he be, Omar thought? It was a stupid thought, and one he'd remember for years. He'd remember his own dumb self as he turned around and started to walk fast, then run, until the corner and the long hot stretch of suburbia. He found an open yard with a side path and turned into it. The crack of thunder and the way he jerked, scared of something and nothing. He remembered it all, the grass smelling of fresh rain and breathing soil, the small yapping mutt telling him off, the blank faces of the family who watched him run through the back and over the fence towards the creek. The sun had left him and he felt sharp bullets of rain hit his face.

He remembered his breath coming back at him from the cement as his head hit the back paving of the yard, the cops tackling him down, their rattling voices and perfumed sweat. Thunder, the sky emptying itself over him till his mouth was full of brown water. Malik, he remembered thinking, you bastard with your bragging Facebook page, what made me post on your wall after so long? Malik, you've left a hole in me.

10

Paddington

Iris Street was quiet and leafier than I'd expected. But of course this was fifty years after the fact and Paddington is not the slum it used to be.

I'd walked downhill past the walls of Victoria Barracks and the pokey local library where they'd helped me with the old photos. The morning had been hazy and by midday my shirt was glued to me. Outside Victoria Barracks, a couple of off-duty servicemen were waiting for a lift somewhere. They had crisp shirts, khaki backpacks and pink damp cheeks.

A building site behind the service station was sending a plume of cement dust into the air. One of the workers was on his break, sitting on the kerb sucking on a cigarette through his blackened fingers and gulping a yellow sports drink. It was only a few metres before I'd turned the corner and was enveloped by the hush of mature fig trees. The tree roots had broken the footpath, which hung open in chunks like torn liquorice. Cicadas were an eerie alarm in my ears.

In Iris Street, there was discussion going on at the door of number 8, where a courier was trying to make a delivery. Wrong address, it seemed. A large man stood in the doorway peering at the name on the address label. From inside his tiny house, a stereo pumped out indifferent 1980s pop music. Even from three metres away, I could see over their shoulders back through the house to the sliding door leading to the yard, sunshine through cigarette smoke, a tiny living room with DVDs stacked against the walls.

The narrow street fell down towards the Moore Park sports complexes. Overhanging paperbark trees, smaller cousins to the figs, dampened noise and soaked up the glare that fell unfiltered back up on Oxford Street. They'd grown to the point where they formed a canopy above the street. A bit different from old photos of bleak Depression era doorways I'd found in the local library. The voices of the men in the doorway bounced around the amphitheatre.

Number 10 was a flat-faced brown house with TEN spelt out in letters on the door. It had the type of security grille you see protecting run-down convenience stores. It was hard to see if anyone was home. In the 1950s there would have been housewives leaning in their doorways, aproned, barefooted kids and cats stalking the footpaths.

Eventually, the business with the parcel was sorted out and the door of number 8 slammed shut. Pushing up against number 10, I brazenly peered through the narrow window. There was a dining table, neatly furnished in a modern spare style, not a metre inside. If luck had been against me, I could have been caught spying on the occupants having a late lunch. But there was no one. From the window, it was impossible to see through to the back. It'd be modern now. There'd be a snug bathroom, an eat-in kitchen, maybe some kid's cubbyhole bedroom with a skylight.

'They're at work,' a voice behind me said. A wide woman with an unbrushed helmet of blonde hair was watching me. She wheezed as she paused between words, shifting in slippers with socks underneath, her upper body clothed only in a saggy singlet top. In one hand, she had a chipped breakfast bowl and in the other two bottles filled with water which leaked down her elbow.

'You know them?' I asked.

'You're new here,' she answered, squinting up at me.

I shed my damp jacket and laughed. 'I suppose people coming and going.'

'They're new, these ones. Only been here three months or so. Always out.'

'You know when they might come in?'

'You been jogging?'

'It's hot.'

'Summer.' She ran her eyes down my black skirt and the too tight top I'd mistakenly worn. Who did she think I was? Reporter maybe.

'If you're looking for a history angle, don't bother.' She made a pretence of shuffling off. 'Not many of the old lot left.'

'You sound like you've seen a few come and go.'

'Should have. I was born in this street.'

I imagined a home birth with women running to and fro with sheets and pales of water. The doors were so close, the noise of a birth would echo back and forth across the narrow canyon of the street.

'Went to school up there at St Ansell's, worked for years down at the Heinz spaghetti factory before it closed. Did my back in, and I still think it was the bending over the belt that did it. I don't suppose I need to use this today, but the strays, someone's got to help them.' She clutched the bottles and bowl awkwardly against her chest, about to drop them all. She went on about the cats and the council, her voice settling into a rattling consistency.

There was nowhere to put down the papers except on the car bonnet in front of me. I dumped them there, hoping it wasn't her car. Above us, a few noisy miners were fighting in the paperbark trees. There was another dump of rain coming.

One of the bottles slipped and I grabbed at it, sending a delightful stream of water down my legs.

'Oh, bloody bottles, just look at that mess!' She looked me up and down, longer than she needed to. It was only water. 'Those shoes'll be filled with it.'

'Oh, it's OK.'

'Come in, luv, and I'll give you a towel.' She handed me the second bottle while she pulled back the screen door.

Getting my jacket, I glanced down the narrow gap between the houses. You'd be able to hear every word uttered by next door. An argument would be noise pollution.

My feet stepped into a sponge of 1970s carpet. A long cord dangled from the vertical blind at the back of the small room which was both hall and living room. Without looking, I knew the rest. The small bedroom to the right, then the old kitchen at the back which gave onto the laneway. A cat was skulking among the potted rosebushes in the yard.

Old newspapers, packed in plastic bags, crowded the mean kitchen table. A statue of a rustic girl, lurid pink blooms in her hair, threatened to fall from the top of the fridge where it was wedged against a colony of plastic containers. An overripe melon, hidden somewhere, flooded the room with an overpowering sweetness.

'I'll get that towel. Take a seat.' Indicating a sagging couch with foam issuing from its seat, she wheezed off.

'Look, really, it's fine,' I called after her, reluctant to sit. 'I'm Kate, by the way.'

'You can't walk in those shoes, luv. What's wrong with you girls these days? No sense.' I suppose anyone under the age of fifty was a 'girl' to her.

'Not many reporters get this close to the action, right?' A hard laugh echoed from the tiny bedroom. She knew about it then.

'Oh, I'm not a reporter,' I called out.

She emerged and handed me a bedraggled towel.

'Well, not a formal reporter, like from TV or news.'

'But you did come about the house next door – I saw you spying in.' An eagerness burnt in her eyes.

'It's more a private thing.' If anything like a murder can be private. The street would have been packed with cops, the wives at the doors, the cats weaving between the legs of the onlookers.

'Doing some uni project, eh? I've had a few of those – sociology or some rubbish.'

'Just a friend of the family.'

Shuffling closer, she examined my face, the odour of sour milk drifting from her lips. I pressed the towel into the shoe. Moisture warmed my fingers as I worked it, still standing.

'Sit down,' she said. 'You look done in.'

The couch sunk under me. I sat forward and felt the steel struts of the thing under my thighs. I'd turned into one of those old door-to-door salesmen trying to clinch a deal.

'So you know about the incident next door? Years back.'

'Saw it all, luv.' She fumbled for a packet of cigarettes on a side table and lit up. 'Helping me mum with the washing. After work and hot as Hades inside, so was glad to be wetting my arms.'

'I just can't imagine…' I shook my head.

'Yes you can, why else you here?'

'Oh, but seeing it, experiencing that kind of event…'

'Event? It wasn't a radio show or something on the telly.'

'Turn of phrase, you know…'

'Sometimes I think it just happened yesterday – Mum and Dad are gone now. They made sense of it somehow. Well, they alway do, mums and dads, don't they?' She smiled, glancing at me wistfully. 'Now it's just me and the cats. I knew their mums too and their grandmums.' She nodded towards the growing pride of cats between the roses.

An eerie dark started to fall as clouds thickened. The patch of weed sprouting between the cracked pavers was a lurid green.

There was a rap from the front door.

'June? You in?' The woman had no need to yell into the tiny space.

June got up and let her in.

She was June's age. Thin, her eyes watery blue, her chest sunk beneath a floral polyester blouse. There were cigarette stains on her fingers. 'Oh,' she said seeing me sitting with the shoe in my hand.

'She came to look at the house, Mazie. Family friend.'

June grabbed the damp shoe and continued with the towelling. I found my toes curling into the carpet, and wondered what decade old decay I was mining.

'I found these outside.' Mazie waved the wad of papers I'd left on the car bonnet. 'You haven't fed them yet, have you, June?'

Mazie meant the cats. June rose and rattled some cans of food down from a cupboard.

'So you knew the family then?' asked Mazie.

'Kind of.'

'Plenty of noise from the house. People coming and going.'

'He was a strange bloke,' June chimed in. 'Wasn't he, Mazie?'

The police thought they were both strange. Both of their files were still restricted. I gnawed at my lower lip.

'And what happened to them?' I blurted out.

The women stopped, looked at each other.

'There were ambulances, cops, all sorts.'

'They had a daughter,' I said, watching them both. My mother, who suicided in a high security unit at St Vincent's. I was in foster care by then.

June nodded slowly as if she also was thinking of her. 'Poor kid. I went to see her once. Tried to talk to her. She didn't know me from Adam.'

'You were here, weren't you? You must have seen them…abscond.' There was no other word for it. Fled, leaving their daughter and grand-daughter alone with the blood.

'Sound like the cops. You sure you're not one of them?'

I shrugged, smiled. They could think what they liked. I'd been trac-ing these people for years. The possible sightings in Queensland, some squat near Bellingen, a TAB in Broken Hill. The police had given up. I imagined them holed up in a rusted combi van selling illegal grog. I had no memory of him. All I remembered of my grandmother were two steel grey eyes.

A lightness had appeared in June's eyes. 'It's all right, my dears,' she said, handing Mazie my shoe and pulling open the tin. 'That was all years ago. They're long gone.'

'A mess, and a shame. Other people.'

'She's passed on now – the daughter. It's over.'

I wanted to slap her face but instead folded and refolded my pa-pers.

They went to the yard and I followed them. A drain gurgled uncov-ered up against the wall. A handful of mean curtain windows watched over the yard from the houses on the other side of the laneway. The cats were everywhere. As I watched, a tortoiseshell clambered awkwardly over the palings and fell to the ground with a muffled thud.

June opened the gate into the laneway and another woman entered the yard. She was a harassed sandy woman with old-fashioned orange lipstick and wild red hair.

'A lady's here, Margaret,' said Mazie. 'About the house. Wanting to know about it, the murder.' At least she could say the word.

Margaret peered at me and brushed a strand of hair out of her eyes. 'Nice to have visitors.'

The other two cackled but I didn't get the joke.

'So was it out there they left it?' I asked, indicating the alleyway.

'You mean the axe?' asked Margaret. 'Come on, I'll show you.' She took my hand and escorted me to the lane as if I were blind. 'Hanging there.' She pointed to the spot and went on in the hushed tone of a haunted house tour guide. 'Between the palings. The very same one he used for doing the wood. He was a skilled axeman. He entered the Royal Easter Show once, I believe. Didn't get a ribbon, though.'

Back in the yard, the cats were trailing off and cleaning themselves after the feed. The women stopped whispering.

'You been on TV?' Mazie asked. '*60 Minutes* maybe.'

'Who was he? The...' I asked. The body. There was no facial reconstruction in those days.

'Some fella – there were few of them called into the house, you know. Always trouble. SP bookie stuff maybe.'

'The police files – it says they got in a car out there, in the lane.'

'Got clear away. That's what someone said.'

'Who was that?'

She shrugged.

Drops of water hitting my scalp told me a storm was coming. June had dropped my shoe amidst the cats. They swarmed over it, around it, it toppled and became smothered with their soft poundings. June sloshed water into the bowls. I searched and searched my mind – there was the smell of boiled cabbage, a damp cot, dawn skies. I must have been there that day. Sleeping metres away.

'I might have to go back inside, sit down,' I said.

'You're still done in, luv,' said June. 'Maybe a lie down.'

'Why an axe?' I asked. 'Why did they use that on him?'

'He worked on the railways,' said June. 'Always breaking up old sleepers.'

'Remember the kitten, June?' Margaret looked gleeful. 'When he did for that kitten with the axe?'

'He was always chopping something – suppose it came natural.'

'It was a ginger, it was,' said Margaret. 'A great-uncle of one of these.'

'Don't, Margaret,' said Mazie. 'I'd forgotten all about that.'

I took a deep breath to steady myself. Reaching amongst the swirl of cats, I grabbed my shoe and shoved it back onto my foot.

'They never found the whole body, though, did they? Only hair and blood.'

'You've done your homework, haven't you?'

'I've been researching this for years.'

'You've taken your time – coming here, I mean.'

'I've been putting it off – coming to the actual place, coming…' I was about to say 'coming back' but stopped myself.

The gate opened again. Who now? Another grey-haired woman was coming through to the lane. She hesitated, blinked in the rain, her thin arm keeping the gate open. Her name was Lil. The wind gusted and tugged at Lil's hair. The cats started to dart and climb, a pair fell and tumbled in a mock fight.

The women looked at Lil then back towards me.

It was Margaret who spoke first. 'It's not *60 Minutes*, is it? You aren't on TV. It's something else – I've seen you before.'

Lil's fingers formed a claw along the rusty frame of the gate.

'Look, Lil,' said Mazie. 'Look at her – she's like little Katrina. She's like…' She reached out to stroke my chin just as she had with the cats.

Instinctively, I pulled back. The papers were with me and I scrambled to save them from the pool of water expanding at my feet. All my thoughts, my musings, my dogged years of searching. Those papers were everything to me. I'd spent ten years looking for this grandmother, the woman who'd cared for me, the closest thing to a mother I'd ever had, until that day. I seemed to be surrounded by them, these cat women, these aproned matrons.

Lil started walking towards me slowly, and then with a hurried wading sound of dislodged water. She clutched at the air between us as if a curtain hung invisible there and she was tearing it away. There was terror and some private agony in her eyes. A scream escaped me.

Hurrying back into the house, a cat shrieked as I stood on its tail. My breath sounded in the humid rooms, I sped through the gloomy kitchen, to the front door where the real world of the street waited for me. I slammed the door. The papers were turning to mush in my hands.

A pair of feet shuffled at the front door behind me, then a voice.

'Katrina?'

I glanced at her and something shifted in me. 'This is mad.' My voice wasn't my own. It was some forlorn child's.

'It is you – Katrina?'

'Why? I don't…get it. Are you…?'

'Katrina, it IS you, oh my, oh dear.' She started giggling.

'I was fostered out. I was given up.'

'I didn't mean to lose you both. I've been waiting for years. Waiting and waiting. I knew one day…'

'Those women – they…what did they do?'

'Old friends. They always help each other out. They saved my life dear. I went to school with them – we've always lived in Iris Street.'

'Why didn't you just leave him?'

'And leave my friends?'

There was no mistaking the grey eyes. She stepped onto the kerb. She only came up to my shoulders, her tight little mouth was my own. So who did it then? Who used the axe and killed my grandfather? Her friend June? But no, looking into her eyes, I knew it wasn't the work of a friend.

'I don't believe it,' I muttered, dragging shaking fingers through my hair.

She laughed with her head back, her eyes aflame, hard lines rising from her thin cheeks.

'What's so funny?' I asked.

'You're like your mum – squeamish.'

'She had a break down after…what you did.'

'Come in and have tea, luv. June's putting the kettle on.'

'You're…' A monster, I wanted to say. Maybe he'd made her one, but did that matter now?

'I miss your mum every day, Katrina dear. She was a bit weak, like him. But you're different.' She smiled and went to touch my cheek. 'And now you're mine again.'

'Don't touch me!' I screamed.

I grabbed my papers and started to walk as fast as I could back up and out of the street. Thunder rumbled overhead and I felt a river of damp air dragging at me. My papers fell and I let them tumble into the growing pool of drain water as I hurried away.

'I'll never let you go now, Katrina,' she yelled. The storm roared above, but not enough to obliterate the sound of the woman. 'Never.'